Hunter
in the Dark

DEAR TRACEY
I`WANT TO SAY MERRY CHRISTMAS
AND WONDERFUL NEW YEAR , HEALTH,
AND TO SEE YOU IN 2019 AT THE NEW
LOCATION

Hunter
in the Dark

MONICA HUGHES

Fitzhenry & Whiteside

Fitzhenry & Whiteside, 195 Allstate Parkway, Markham, Ontario L3R 4T8
In the United States, 311 Washington Street, Brighton, Massachusetts 02135

www.fitzhenry.ca   godwit@fitzhenry.ca

Fitzhenry & Whiteside acknowledges with thanks the Canada Council for the Arts,
the Government of Canada through the Book Publishing Industry Development
Program (BPIDP), the Ontario Arts Council and the Government of Ontario
through the Ontario Media Development Corporation's Ontario Book Initiative
for their support for our publishing program.

10 9 8 7 6 5 4 3

National Library of Canada Cataloguing in Publication
Hughes, Monica, 1925-2003
Hunter in the dark / Monica Hughes.

ISBN 1-55005-056-7
I. Title.
PS8565.U34H8 2003   jC813'.54   C2003-900593-3
PZ7.H87364Hu 2003

Design and Layout: Tanya Montini for TM+CO.
Cover image: Don Kilby Illustration
Printed and bound in Canada

For Russ, who hunts in the light;
and in memory of Russell Avey
who was not afraid of the dark.

— *M.H.*

AUTHOR'S NOTE

Although this story is set in Alberta, I have ignored
the existence of the W.W. Cross Institute for reasons
which the plot development will make clear.

ONE

Mike Rankin geared down to a correct fifty kilometres an hour and slid quietly into Barrhead. The town was barely awake, but the lights in a small café were tempting. He thought of hot coffee. He wanted it so badly he could smell it, and his foot touched the brake.

He had almost come to a stop when he saw the RCMP car parked at the curb, and his foot moved automatically from brake to gas pedal. He picked up speed and drove smoothly through the town. His palms were sweating against the wheel, and he rubbed them, one at a time, against his thighs.

There was nothing unusual about the truck, he told himself firmly. It was just a dun-coloured, four-wheel-drive Toyota. They were as thick as fleas on a bear's back in the north. Nothing noticeable about it. About him. He took a deep breath and began to whistle between his teeth, willing his thumping heart into quietness.

For a moment the fear had jolted him into that other world, the one most people lived in, but soon the familiar feeling of separateness was back. It gave him a comfortable feeling of invisibility. So long as he didn't feel part of their world, he wasn't.

The sun rose in the southeast behind his left shoulder, a red ball bouncing up suddenly into the cold November sky. The shadow of the pickup rippled over the frost heaves in the road ahead. Then the trees began to close in again on either side, the pines and spruces greyed with a dusting of snow, the poplars gaunt, a few golden leaves still hanging like forgotten banners.

Half an hour later the sun was properly up, a brilliant gold and comfortably hot on the back of his neck. Fort Assiniboine on his right. Not long now. Just another eight kilometres or so ... on the left ... there it was. Highway 658. Off the paved road and onto gravel.

He glanced at the dashboard. It was 8:28 Saturday morning. After that party the parents wouldn't even be up themselves, and when they did wake up they'd be sure to let him sleep in. It would be at least four hours before they found out that he wasn't in his bed, and who knows how much longer before they discovered the note under the pillow.

He felt a twinge of guilt and pushed it to the back of his mind. It was like during the war – kids enlisting because they felt they had to, no matter how much their mothers cried and carried on. This was the same. This was his own private war. He hoped they'd understand.

He pulled the truck over onto the shoulder and dug out the sketch map that Doug had given him. About three kilometres along this road, after he crossed the bridge over the Freeman River, there should be a fire road slashed through the forest. He drove slowly, watching the odometer. There it was, running uphill on his right, a ruler-straight cut of white snow against the crowding dark of the trees. He had to drive up the fire road for about ten kilometres until it was intersected by an old seismic cut running due north and south. Go north, Doug had told him, and he'd find a perfect place to camp far from interfering eyes, down in the valley of the Freeman River.

There'd be good water down there, not like the Athabasca, which might look milky clear, but which was already fouled with all the junk from every little town and village between the Columbia Icefield and Fort Assiniboine. But the Freeman was just a little river rising in the middle of the Swan Hills, and that was wild country. Bear country, not people country.

Mike turned right, geared down and began to climb. The snow was no problem. In fact it made driving a bit easier, smoothing out the bumps and filling in some of the holes. The Toyota took the slope and the rough terrain valiantly. Once Mike was over the crest of the hill and could no longer be seen from the main road he stopped the pickup and got out to stretch his legs and look around.

He stood on a ridge of land that ran upwards, northwest, rounded like the back of a great sleeping animal, an animal whose muscles rippled beneath a dense fur of spruce, pine and poplar. As far as he could see, ahead and to the right and left, the forest lay thick and solid. Behind him, to his right, he could see a haze over Fort Assiniboine. It was very quiet up here on the fire road. The air was cold and clean and above him the sky had the same freshness, a piercing, transparent blue-green that went on forever.

Mike felt like yelling out loud with triumph. He'd done it! He'd got clean away. He'd outwitted the lot of them. Thinking about it was marvellous, but scary too. There was so much that could still go wrong. He had to keep his head, not let this feeling, a bit like being drunk, get in the way of his judgement. He had to remember everything he'd learned in Forestry Conservation, at the Gun Club, from Doug and Doug's dad.

He wished, with a small pang of regret, that *his* dad felt the way he did about the bush, so that they could have shared all this together, before it was too late. But then, Mike reasoned, Dad would probably have insisted on coming along, and this was something he had to do by himself. So it was probably all for the best, the way things were.

He walked back a few steps to the brow of the hill where he could see the deep crimped pattern of tires running downhill to the road. He hoped it would snow again soon. Just a skiff, just enough to dust over the pickup's tread marks, so that there would be no sign of him at all, as if he didn't exist.

As if ... he turned his thoughts away like a skater turning back from a dark patch of mushy ice. He walked back and climbed into the pickup, rubbed his hands together to warm them, shifted into gear and drove carefully along the fire road northwest towards the Swan Hills.

He drove slowly with one eye on the odometer — 11.2 kilometres. There it was, running north and south at an angle to the fire road, a seismic cut made by some oil exploration crew. Northwards it led downhill towards the river valley. He couldn't actually see the river from up here, but he could see the shadow of the crease it had made in the land. The cut was old. Saplings and spruce seedlings had sprung up in the open space, poking up through the shallow snow cover, hiding the deep scars of cat treads.

He went down cautiously, but the pickup was high off the ground and the tallest poplar saplings just bent and brushed it underneath. It took him a lurching fifteen minutes to negotiate the steep slope down to the river, and he was sweating before he got there. But it was worth it. The river ran clean and cold and fast, too fast to have frozen yet, except right at the edges in the shallows among the weeds.

Mike turned the pickup carefully in among the trees, so that it was hidden from casual eyes, and switched off the engine. There were the small popping noises of the hot engine beginning to cool. Then the silence crowded in, a silence so profound that he felt that he must have gone deaf.

He strained to hear, but there was nothing but the roaring of his own blood in his ears, the sound of his own breathing. He made himself relax, and slowly he began to hear again. A soft background sound that was the voice of the river. Down here close to the river the air was still, but high above him a sudden winter wind rattled the dead poplar leaves against their branches. He could hear chickadees over there in that big spruce close to the water ... dee dee ... chickadee ... dee dee. Startlingly sudden and as loud as a rattle at a football game, a squirrel scolded him for invading its territory.

He suddenly felt very tired, but he made himself get down and walk along the bank of the river, away from the man-made seismic cut that ended in a cruel mangling of the river bank. He walked slowly, looking for the perfect camp-site – just one more look, the next place might be a little better – until he made himself stop. There was no point having to haul everything a kilometre through the bush from the truck.

Then he stumbled on it, a small clearing with a southeast exposure where the river made a sudden loop northwards. Perfect.

It took him three trips to haul the tent, the sleeping bag and air mattress, and the backpack crammed with supplies and a change of clothes. By the time he'd made the last trip his knees were trembling, but he forced himself to go on laying out the tent, pushing the rods into place, hammering pegs into the hard ground, tightening the guy ropes. He placed the tent with its door to the south and its back to the northern loop of the river, and he blew up the air mattress with what seemed like the very last of his breath, and shook out the downfilled bag and laid it on top.

His body begged for rest, but it was cold, and he was hungry as well as tired. He laid the gun in its case carefully along the inside wall of the tent, and began to make a fire.

There was a huge stone in the clearing that was perfect for a reflector, and he cleared the snow away from in front of it, scraped away the matted layer of grass and weeds, and laid his fire on the bare ground. There was no need to search for wood. Just cleaning up the deadfall in the clearing gave him a good pile.

By the time he'd scrambled down the bank to the river and filled his saucepan with icy water the fire was burning bright and hot. Coffee first. He could hardly wait for the water to boil. A mug full to the brim, blazing hot with a big dollop of sugar for quick energy. His hand shook so much that he spilled the first mouthful.

By the time the first mugful had gone down he had enough energy to dig out the frying pan from his backpack and put bacon on to cook. Then two eggs, spattering hot fat as he broke them into the pan, and a slice of fried bread to mop up the bacon grease. Another mug of coffee.

"That's better," he said out loud. "I think I might live." He grinned at his private joke, got up and stretched. Was there something magic about the bush, or was it his own cooking? He couldn't remember a meal ever tasting that good. He put the food away in the backpack and used a length of rope chucked over a high poplar branch to hoist the pack high above his head, away from marauding bears.

Only then did he crawl into the tent, taking off his boots at the door, and lie down with a contented sigh on the top of his sleeping bag. The sun glanced into the tent, low in the southeastern sky, just grazing the tree tops. He lay on his back, his stomach full and warm, his arms and legs throbbing with fatigue. He could hear his heart banging against his ribs. He felt half triumphant, half scared. The sun began to warm the inside of the tent like a gentle sauna. He drifted into sleep.

Mike's sleep was filled with hospital noises: the clatter of metal trolleys on tiled floors, the continuous push-sigh of swing doors, the chatter of the paging system ... Doctor Richards to O.R.... Inhalation Therapy to Room 302 ... Doctor Blackett to Station 41.... He twitched and then lay still. Sweat trickled from his forehead and darkened the blond hair at his temples. They were coming at him with a needle now, a perfectly enormous needle. They were holding him down, and he was fighting, yelling, begging them to leave him alone. His body was filled with liquid fire and agony. He rolled over onto his side, curled up into a tight ball. He groaned, and woke up to the sound of his own voice.

"Oh, my God!" He brought up one hand, heavy as lead, to wipe the sweat off his face and neck. The lights were too bright. He could see them through his eyelids, blood-red. He opened his eyes slowly, reluctantly, to find that he was looking into a brilliant triangle of light. The sun was shining full into the tent, turning it into an oven.

He sat up, his head swimming with sleep, and skinned out of his jacket. Phew! Some dream! But only a dream. That was all over, all in the past. *Now* was where he had to be.

He crawled over to the tent door and poked his head out. The chickadees were still busy, tweaking at pine seeds and berries. The water chuckled at some private joke in the loop of the river behind him. It was all so beautifully uncomplicated, it made his dream seem even more bizarre. He put his boots on and found that he was thinking about lunch.

He looked at his watch. Incredible! He'd been asleep for almost four hours. He hunkered down by the pink-ashed remains of the fire, feeding it small pieces of dry wood and blowing them into life. Just a light lunch, he decided. Soup, bread and cheese, and an apple. He'd really spread himself at dinner.

Doug had helped him buy supplies, freeze-dried camping stuff; but he had also raided the family freezer, and he'd picked out a package of three T-bone steaks. They'd stay frozen all right, tucked away in the backpack up in the shelter of the poplar tree, and he'd be careful to burn the bones and scraps so as not to give the Swan Hill grizzlies any ideas.

Three days. And after that what? He couldn't stay away forever. Or could he? It was a tempting thought, something he'd have to work on later when he had time. But first he'd make lunch, and then have a scout around to see if the game was really as good as Doug had made out.

He boiled water and spilled into it a package of freeze-dried soup. Bean and bacon, the package said. While it slowly swelled into life, sitting in its pot at the edge of the fire, he buttered bread and cut thick slices of cheese. He pulled over a dry log for a seat, and sat in the sun sipping his soup and munching the cheese sandwich.

There wasn't a breath of wind and the sun gently heated the little clearing. He was amazingly warm even in his shirtsleeves. Just right. And the soup was just right too. Great, in fact. He took his time, chewing the sharp cheddar and breaking off little corners of crust for the chickadees. They hopped excitedly from branch to branch above him, egging each other on until one, braver than the rest, landed in his open palm and snatched a crust. The tiny weight and the cold hard feet surprised Mike. The sharp eyes looked at him unwinkingly, the black-capped head tilted to one side. Then it flew away and another came, and then another, until the crusts were gone. He drank the last of the soup and fished out the bits at the bottom with a finger. Delicious.

He washed up breakfast and lunch together. It didn't take long, just a dip in the river. The plate was a bit streaky, but that didn't matter. Maybe after dinner he'd heat some water and have a proper clean-up. He got a big foil-wrapped potato out of the backpack and buried it under the hot ashes of the fire, using a stick and the point of his knife, and raking the hot cinders back on top.

He fussed around, putting everything away, the food safely out of bear reach, the other things neatly in the tent. He put on his mackinaw and the Blaze Orange jacket and cap that Doug had lent him. The compass was on its string around his neck, tucked into his breast pocket. The emergency kit was in his side pocket, out of the way.

After he picked up his gun he felt an odd reluctance to

leave this cosy camp. What was the matter with him? He'd been waiting for this all year. Anyway, all he was going to do was scout around, see if he could recognize the deer trails Doug had described to him, and then work out a plan for tomorrow. That's all he was going to do. He put the gun down again, slipped it behind his air mattress, just in case some stranger should come snooping around his camp.

A last look around, ridiculously it felt like leaving home, and then he set off, angling uphill away from the river almost due west. Walking was difficult at first. The trees were crowded close and the spaces between them seemed interlaced with deadfall and brush. Then he came across a deer run going more or less in the same direction. It was a deer run, wasn't it?

The snow had been worn away to the soft padding of pine and spruce needles beneath. It was easier to be quiet walking along this faint dark line instead of breaking through the brush. He practised putting his feet down carefully, heel first, rolling slowly onto the toe and only then moving his weight forward and taking the weight off his back foot. He stopped every few minutes and looked around. There were places just below shoulder height where the tree bark was scarred, where antlers had been scraped and scratched to get rid of the annoying tatters of velvet.

Then he saw a hoofprint. Whitetail or mule deer – he didn't know enough to tell the difference. But there it was, neatly planted in a fresh drift of snow, exactly the way it had looked in the book. His heart pounded as he straightened his back and looked slowly round. The forest seemed very still and empty. Even the chickadees were silent.

He walked forward and, sudden as a burglar alarm, there came the rattling chitter of a squirrel right above his head. He jumped and then stood still, willing it to be silent. That sound must have travelled for kilometres, he thought. He listened and imagined that he could hear the forest listening back. The squirrel quietened and in the tense silence he moved on, even more carefully.

He had walked and waited and looked and listened for over an hour before he came to a place where the deer runs seemed to converge together, to head downhill towards one particular spot. He followed one of the trails curiously. When he stopped to listen he could hear the sound of water. A little farther, and he came out of the trees beside the river. Across its width the hill rose steep and dark, but on this side the frozen marsh made a firm place for the deer to come down to drink.

And not only deer. The overnight skiff of snow had dusted the river bank with white, and clearly marked in it were the dog-like prints of a wolf or coyote, paw marks of some small fur-bearing animal – a mink or ermine maybe – and the hoppity prints of a snowshoe rabbit, the huge rear feet splayed out ahead of the tiny front paws. In one place there were the unmistakeable fat footprints of a bear. Black or grizzly? A grizzly's would be much larger than a black bear's – but what was "larger"? These looked enormous. Lines from *The Hunter Training Manual* drifted into his mind.

He almost invariably flees at the sight or sound of man, but has been known to injure or even kill them, generally only when provoked. Their disposition is unpredictable and all grizzlies should be treated with respect.

Almost invariably. Generally. Really comforting generalizations, Mike thought. He stared at the huge prints, the claws so clearly imprinted in the snow.

He pulled himself together. The footprints weren't going to attack him, that was sure. The bear had come to the river, drank its fill and gone. So why was he standing here getting hysterical? The odds against being killed by a bear, in fact the odds against even meeting one, were far greater than the odds that were on him already. Dumb.

He became suddenly aware that the sun had dropped, with the abruptness of winter, behind the hills to the southwest, and that a chill wind was stirring the dead leaves and frozen rushes of the marsh. Cold night air poured down into the valley. He shivered and set out briskly along the river bank towards his camp. At least he'd made a start. Next time out he'd bring his gun. Odds or not, he was beginning to feel very uncomfortable in grizzly country without a rifle.

Back in camp he scrambled out of his hunting jacket and into his downfill. Then he took the cover off the axe and cut all the deadfall he had already collected into neat, foot-long pieces. That warmed him up all right. When the fire was going again he set the frying pan on the coals to get good and hot. From his backpack he got out a steak, an onion and a package of mushrooms. It was already almost dark, and he had to use the flashlight to see what he was doing, not to slice off a finger instead of the onion.

By the time the steak had defrosted enough to put in the pan, the onion was a bit overcooked, but that didn't matter, he decided. In fact the burned bits tasted like caramel, sweet rather than oniony. He dug the potato out of the red-hot ashes and picked open the foil with the point of his knife. Perfect. He burned his fingers squeezing it open, plopping a big hunk of butter into the steaming white of the inside.

He ate the steak slowly, savouring each juicy mouthful and the tangy taste of the burnt fat at the edges. He sucked the bone, ripping off the last shreds of meat with his front teeth. Then the hot potato, and the mushrooms and onions all mixed together. Real gourmet stuff.

For dessert he opened a can of pears, fishing them right out of the can with his fingers and then slurping down the juice to top off the meal. Man, that was good!

He threw all the remains into the hot fire to kill the food smells, repacked everything except the coffee and the sugar, and hoisted the pack up into the bear-proof poplar. Then he stretched, looked around his camp site and gave an enormous satisfied belch. It was pitch dark now except for the circle of golden light around the fire. As the flames rose and fell the darkness oozed like molasses from between the trees and reached out towards him, only to be pushed back again when the flames flickered high once more.

The sky was black too, but it held a different kind of blackness, an empty dark rather than the solid dark of the forest. In the emptiness the stars shone with the cold brilliance of polished steel. He could see the three stars of Orion's Belt in the southeast just above the clearing. They'd never seemed so bright.

Reluctantly Mike stepped out of the golden circle that the fire made, the circle where he felt safe. Outside it the darkness seemed to close eagerly around him, and the fire dwindled to a tiny gold spark, a pathetically small light in the enormousness of the dark forest and the dark sky.

He peed against a tree and hurried back shivering. He piled his newly cut firewood close to the tent and made up the fire so that the flames rose high. He took off his boots and left them just inside the tent. Then he skinned out of his outer clothes and dived into the sleeping bag in his thermal t-shirt and longjohns. Gosh, it was icy down there at the bottom!

He rolled over onto his left side so that he could see the comforting firelight just beyond the triangle of the door. Where was the flashlight? There. Close to his hand. And the rifle behind him along the back wall of the tent. No sweat. He shut his eyes and firmly told himself to go to sleep.

Behind his shut lids the dark came crowding in.... The nights had always been the worst. At night the thoughts that he could usually keep at bay during the day began to slink past his weakened defenses, like hungry wolves sneaking past a dying fire.

In all the months of planning that had gone into this final adventure he had never once realized how long the winter nights would be ... the nights that he would have to spend alone. The early November sun had set at 5:01 and would not rise again until 7:36. That worked out to more than fourteen hours of night, hours which he could not push back, as he so often did at home, by switching on his bedside lamp and reading a spy story, or by putting on his earphones and tuning in to K97, or by catching a late movie on television. There had always been something he could use to turn away the dark, turn away his thoughts about the dark.

But not out in the bush. There was the fire, but that wasn't enough. In fact, by its very act of dying down it made the dark seem even closer and more real.

Well, he was here, and there was nothing he could do about it now. He lay cocooned in his sleeping bag, his knees bent, his arms hugging his chest, and let the dark come ... the anger, the frustration, and then the cold fear that was like a sickness itself. It was always the same. In the end it went away, leaving him weak and trembling. But it did go. The thing to remember was that it never did go on forever.

He relaxed cautiously and opened his eyes. The remains of the fire gave off a red-gold glow, reflected off the big stone right into the tent. He could feel the warmth on his face like comforting hands. Slowly the heat began to seep down into his arms and shoulders, his body, his legs, even his toes.

He sighed and lifted a lazy arm to look at the time: 10:37. Well, the parents would certainly know by now what he had done. The question was, would they leave him in peace or would they start combing the country for him?

And what about Doug? Doug was the only person who knew exactly where he was, and why. Would he be able to hold out against the barrage of questions, even threats? Good old Doug, he thought. Hang on, fella. And he drifted off to sleep in the middle of the thought: I'm lucky to have a friend like Doug ... lucky ...

Two

"Boy, you sure are lucky," Doug had told him on his fifteenth birthday, when he saw the stereo tape deck that had been the parents' present to him. "That must have cost a mint!"

"I guess." Mike didn't think much about money. There always seemed to be plenty of it around. He supposed it *was* kind of a splendid gift. Maybe because of him being an only child. "I'm going to put all my favourite cuts on tapes. Great for parties. Why don't I make some for you while I'm at it?"

"That would be great. Thanks." Doug's freckled face split into a cheerful grin. Mike knew he had just bought a small cassette player with some of the money he'd saved from his dishwashing job at Dinty's, the part he hadn't given to his mom to help out.

Doug was the oldest of seven kids, each of them born about two years apart so that when they were all out walking together they looked like a set of stairs – except that now Doug stood shoulder to shoulder with his dad, and his mother fitted in somewhere between Jonathan and Judy, and, as she complained, seemed to be shrinking daily.

"Serves you right for feeding us all that growing food," Doug said one night when Mike was staying over for dinner. "Chili and apple pie – what do you expect, midgets?"

"Maybe I'll put you all on bread and water and slow you down a bit," she threatened, ladling stew into bowls big enough to bath the baby in.

Mike loved the whole O'Reilly clan. They were curly-haired and wide-grinned and freckled, from Doug all the way down to Sue-Ann. In fact the dog Mutt had the very same grin, only being a hairy sort of beast, any freckles he might have were not visible. But he was still an O'Reilly, and nothing bothered him, not even being tripped over, which happened often enough since he was a clumsy creature and the house was small and crowded, nor having his tail chewed on by Sue-Ann, who was teething.

Mike dug into his stew and looked around. They were eating in the kitchen as usual, since the dining-room table was always littered with projects, from Doug's fly-tying rig to the Meccano pieces that Geoffrey was working on, pages of half-finished homework cheerfully abandoned in favour of the jig-saw puzzle spread across the other end of the table, and a half-eaten peanut butter sandwich that nobody would own up to. Mutt would probably finish it in the end – he was a fiend for peanut butter.

Even with the big dining-room table, projects tended to overflow into the living-room area, and when you sat down you were wise to check behind the cushions. There might be anything stuffed behind them, from Mrs. O'Reilly's knitting to one of Mutt's bones.

The thing about the O'Reilly house, Mike figured, reaching for the pile of bread, was that you didn't have to worry about *things*. At home it was different. At home you lowered your voice and took your shoes off even if it hadn't been raining. At home the living room had an oyster-grey carpet, the chairs and twin loveseats were covered in velvet of a slightly darker grey, and the curtains were of off-white linen with a grey and black thread running through it, an absolute steal, Mrs. Rankin confided, at fifty dollars a metre.

The whole house was always spotless except for Mike's room, which he refused to allow the housekeeper to interfere with, and there was always a bowl of flowers on the low circular table in the middle of the living room. Mike's mother said they made a house look "lived in," and she always insisted on fresh flowers even in the middle of winter when they cost a fortune, flown in from Central America.

Mike looked up the crowded table to where Mrs. O'Reilly was dishing up second helpings. Her arms were like holsters and her dress was strained at every seam, but she had the kind of bosom that little kids dug their heads into when they'd scraped their knees or come last in the three-legged race. She was the biggest hugger on the block.

He suddenly felt disloyal. "You must be so proud of your mother," people would say when her picture was in the paper. And he was. She looked younger than most of the other mothers he knew. She never shamed him by kissing him in front of his friends, nor did she wear awful clothes as some of them did: either far too young, almost as if they were still in high school themselves, or baggy old things that looked as if they'd come from the Salvation Army.

Mike's mother was perfect, always right for every occasion. Fresh and neat and smelling of her special perfume. Mike remembered how he'd loved the smell when he was little, how he'd lean up against her, sniffing, until she laughed and said he was like a puppy. The scent lingered in her room even when she was away, busy with the Arts Society or the Friends of the Opera, or helping with the Heart Fund or the Cancer Drive.

Mrs. O'Reilly had time for none of these things. Maybe it was the difference between seven kids and a dog and a husband who worked out on Refinery Row, and one kid and a husband who put together parcels of land for condominiums and shopping centres and things like that.

Mike had the best of both worlds. He had the freedom of life at the O'Reilly's, the take-it-or-leave-it, unfussy, unpunctual life; then he had the kind of security that went with a home on Adrian Drive, and a mother and dad he was really proud of. He was a lucky guy, he told himself. By grade eleven he had it made, keeping up his grades, on the senior basketball team, and even going out with Gloria Hlady.

"How did you do it, you son of a gun?" Doug punched him in the ribs. They were in the crowd around the pop machine at the September sock-hop, the first event of the year. Mike had gone right up to Gloria, commanding his palms not to sweat, and he'd asked her for the first dance. She'd smiled, "yes" and then danced with him right up to intermission.

"Oh, it's just my dynamic personality, you know," Mike joshed back, and then struggled out of the crowd to where Gloria was sitting. He handed her a can of Seven-Up. Watching her drink it he couldn't believe that she seemed to go for him. She was new at school, she'd only come to Edmonton that fall. She was gorgeous, small and neat, with dark brown hair that hung straight down her back and looked so heavy and silky that you just wanted to pick it up and feel it.... His hands grew sweaty at the thought, and he took a swig from his can of Coke.

Later that evening as he walked her home – it turned out that she lived only six blocks from him – he asked her, "Why me?"

She stopped under a street light and looked up at him seriously – she didn't have much of a sense of humour, he'd already discovered, but who cared, for laughs he could go out with Doug and the gang – and then she said, "You looked so tidy, so all together ... the others seemed such a mess."

He kissed her goodnight on the porch. The light was blazing and so was the one in the living room, but he didn't care. Then he walked the six blocks home feeling ten feet tall. Gloria Hlady liked him! She let him kiss her! She thought he was tidy and all together....

After that evening Mike was especially careful to wash his hair every morning and make sure he had clean socks. Except when he and Doug and Doug's father went camping on the Thanksgiving weekend. Then they relaxed, all guys together. They slept in their underwear and didn't bother to wash more than was absolutely necessary, and Doug's dad didn't shave. It was great forgetting all about school and civilization and the little pressures like not messing up the house and trying to live up to Gloria's expectations.

Mr. O'Reilly had taught the boys everything he knew about hunting, and that was plenty, since he kept the O'Reilly freezer full most of the year. Their one ambition, the thing they'd talked about all summer and fall, was going hunting themselves once they were sixteen. Doug's birthday was on the 14th of October and Mike's was on the 29th. At sixteen you could get an acquisition certificate and own your very own gun. And at sixteen you were old enough to buy a big-game licence.

Over the campfire they talked for the millionth time about what they were going to do. Doug spread out the Alberta Big Game Regulations Map. It was just about falling apart, they'd folded and unfolded it so many times.

"Swan Hills." Doug pointed with a grubby finger. "Dad says it's terrific. Right, Dad?"

Mr. O'Reilly grunted. He was lying on his back with his cap over his eyes.

"How long's the season up there?" Mike rolled over until he could see past Doug's shoulder. "Whew! Man, you stink!"

"You think you smell of roses? More like a bear...."

When they'd finished scuffling the map had another tear. Doug smoothed it out and looked at the tables at the bottom.

"F 350. That's Big Game Zone Five. Whitetail, mule deer ... Shove over, I can't see, you great ox. Whitetail ... November 1st to the 30th. Mule deer ... the same."

"It's not much time."

"How much do you think we need, you jerk, if we go to the right place? One deer each, that's all. If we go the end of November, with the Teachers' Convention we'll have two days plus a weekend. Dad'll get time off, won't you, Dad?"

Mr. O'Reilly snored gently.

"Four whole days, just the three of us!"

"Four days." Mike rolled over onto his back and stared up through the trees, sniffing the sharpness of pine needles and wood smoke. "But suppose we missed.... D'you suppose there's much difference – between the targets at the rifle range and a deer, I mean?"

"Well, a deer's liable to move, isn't it, turkey? But so what? You worry too much, Mike. Look at your scores on the range!"

"Probably just luck." Mike tried to imagine a whitetail head in place of the usual paper target. Could he? "Just luck."

—

But luck was already running out. Right after Thanksgiving he felt rotten, flu or something. He hoped it wasn't mono – what would he tell Gloria? So he kept quiet and hoped it would wear off by his birthday.

At the breakfast table on the 29th were a heap of presents, and the one from Dad was a Weatherby Mark V deluxe bolt action .257 with a 24-inch barrel and a 4X Bushnell scope.

"Dad, thanks! Wow, it's terrific. You didn't have to ... I mean ... well, it's the best!"

"The best's good enough for my boy." Dad smiled all over his face at Mike's delight. "I know it's what you wanted, and the man assured me this was the one. I hope ..."

"It is. It really is." Mike ran his hand over the stock, smooth, with a finish like silk, like Gloria's hair. He sighted along the barrel.

"Oh, Mike, not in the house."

"It's not *loaded*, Mom. Look."

"I should hope not! But it's just the idea. Those poor animals."

"Anita!"

"Oh, Mom!"

"You men," she teased, and her blue eyes twinkled. "Savages at heart, every one of you! It isn't that we need the meat, not like the O'Reillys."

Mike tried to find words for the excitement of the hunt, an excitement that had nothing to do with bloodthirstiness ... but he couldn't explain.

Mother laughed at his expression. "I won't tease you any more. I understand how you feel. Only, you will be careful, won't you?"

"Mom, give me a break, I can handle it. I'm not a kid any more!"

Mother looked wistful. "I know, dear. I can't believe how tall you've grown this past year. But you've thinned out too much."

"I'm okay. Don't worry. I'm taking Vitamin C pills like crazy. Got to be in top shape tomorrow. It's the game against Ashley High, and they *always* win."

"Only not this time, not with my boy on the team." Dad patted his shoulder, and then got to his feet with a grunt. "I'm off. No idea when I'll be home, Anita. Sorry. Big day. Big deal coming off."

Mike had no appetite. The excitement of his birthday and Dad's stupendous gift, he told himself. And Gloria gave him a gold chain. He hadn't expected that much. Maybe things were getting serious ... he hoped. Then he began to worry about her birthday. She was awfully particular. He'd hate to blow it....

The next day he felt really rotten. If it hadn't been for the basketball game he'd have crawled right back into bed. But this was a big game and the team had been putting in extra practices for weeks. And Gloria would be there, to see him win.... He swallowed a glass of orange juice and half a bran muffin and left for school.

He felt better as the day wore on, and by game time he thought he was all right. Mr. McAlister the coach didn't agree. At the end of the first half "Alice" caught him by the shoulder and pulled him to one side. "What's got into you, Mike? Too many late nights? You're dragging, man. If you can't handle it I'll pull you out."

Mike bit his lip. He could see, over the coach's shoulder, Gloria waving at him. He had to play well for her or never look her in the eye again. "I'm fine," he lied. "A bit nervous, maybe. I'll be okay."

"You'd better be, or I'll have your hide." Alice gave him a friendly shove that nearly sent him toppling. The whistle blew and he ran back to his place, determined to do better or die. It wouldn't be so bad to foul up at an away game, but in their own gym, with Gloria – with everybody – watching, well, no way!

He caught Gloria's anxious look as the whistle blew again, and then there wasn't time to think of her any more. He was too busy forcing his body to do things that had seemed effortless a couple of weeks ago. His gym shoes seemed to have lead weights in their soles and his knees were like boiled spaghetti. He botched an easy intercept, and the Ashley centre got the ball again. He missed, thank goodness, and the other forward grabbed it from him. The game flowed down to the Ashley end. The score was 49 to 46 for the visitors. He heard somebody yell, "Get the lead out, Mike!" and then suddenly there were black spots swimming in front of his eyes, and he could feel his face and neck getting colder, as if all the blood was draining down into his gym shoes.

Mike's next view was of the overhead lights in the gym ceiling. He stared at the wire frame protecting the light just above him. What in the world was he doing flat on his back? Had someone tripped him? Odd that he couldn't remember. He pushed himself up on one elbow and the gym spun sickeningly around him.

"Steady." Old Alice was helping him up. "Can you manage? All right. Go and lie down in the locker room." He beckoned to a couple of boys in the nearest bleacher, and feeling like every kind of idiot Mike let himself be led out of the gym. Behind him the whistle blew, feet thudded and squeaked, the crowd on the bleachers roared.

After he'd lain on one of the benches in the locker room for a bit he felt better. He showered and changed and then sat waiting. Damn. What had gone wrong?

"Hey, Mike, what happened?" The team surged through the swirling door into the locker room and crowded around him.

"I dunno. Flu maybe."

"Rotten luck anyway," the captain, Ted Watson, sympathized.

"Did we win?" He was afraid to ask. He wouldn't feel so bad if ....

"Nah. Ashley walked all over us."

"Damn, I'm sorry. Really. I thought I could handle it."

"Not your fault, I guess."

"You'd better believe it." Alice pushed through the sweaty bodies, stood with his hands on his hips. "A team doesn't stand or fall on the performance of one player – or it's not much of a team. It was a good game and you all played ... well, not too badly. Ashley's got a better team, and we're going to have to sharpen up our defense before we meet them again. That's all. You've changed, Mike? Good. Get your jacket and I'll drive you down to the hospital. The rest of you guys shower and get out of here."

"Hospital? But I'm fine, coach, really."

"Maybe. But there's a school board rule. Anyone losing

consciousness during a game on school time has to be checked over."

"But – "

"The school board wouldn't want your parents suing us for neglect, would they? Quit arguing and get your jacket."

Mike felt like an idiot sitting in an examining room at Emergency, being checked over by a keen young doctor while Alice leaned against the white wall of the cubicle looking bored to death.

"I'm all right," he said for the umpteenth time. "It's just a touch of flu."

"Bones aching? Fever?"

Mike nodded. "A little, maybe. I just haven't shaken it off yet, that's all."

"Fine. Lie down." The doctor began to prod Mike's stomach.

"I don't have a stomach ache. No, that doesn't hurt. Really, I'm – "

"Fine. I heard you. Could be rheumatic fever. We'll have a throat swab to be on the safe side. And a couple of blood samples. Nurse!" He opened the door and yelled. Then, "You seem a bit anaemic. Play much sport?"

"Sure."

"Get knocked about much?"

"I wouldn't say so."

"Fighting?" The doctor laid a finger accusingly on Mike's chest.

"No!" Mike felt himself flushing, just as though he *was*

guilty of something. Old Alice had stopped looking bored and was staring at the bruises that the doctor had pointed out. "'They just happen. I guess I knocked against something, you know how you do. You don't even remember, and then a bruise comes up. It happens all the time. No sweat."

The doctor nodded absently and felt Mike's neck. A technician in white with a tray full of bottles appeared at the door. Before Mike had time to protest she had whipped a piece of rubber tubing around his arm and began to draw vial after vial of blood from the vein in his elbow.

"Hey, that's enough. I said I was fine!"

"I'm through." She grinned at him, pushed a wad of gauze against his elbow crease and bent his arm up. "Hold that for a moment, please." She put the vials back on the tray and returned with a band-aid. "It's still oozing a bit, Doctor," she remarked over her shoulder as she fixed the band-aid in place.

"So I see. Get that lot worked up as soon as you can, will you?"

"We've got an awful backlog."

"Nevertheless."

She nodded and left with a glance at Mike that seemed a bit more than casual.

"Can I go home now?" he asked.

"Sure." The doctor seemed suddenly to have lost interest in Mike's body. "Just give me the name and phone number of your family doctor, will you? And that'll be that."

"No chance of suing the school board, eh?" Old Alice joked.

There was a silence. Then, "No, no. His faint had nothing

to do with the game or a blow from another player. Nothing like that. Moral: don't play basketball when you've got flu." The doctor bustled out, leaving Mike to put on his shirt and jacket.

"I'll drive you home. Will anyone be there?"

Mike glanced at the big electric clock on the wall. "I doubt it. But I'm fine."

"Good, then let's be off. Maybe we'll miss the rush." The coach also looked up at the clock. Mike felt guilty again.

They did get stuck in traffic, and it was after five before Alice let him out of the car at the bottom of the driveway. The house was empty and there was a note from Mother on the fridge door.

Mike, I have to go straight from my afternoon with the Auxiliary to dinner at the Plaza. Home late. Steaks are in the meat locker. Mrs. Holden has made salad and dessert for you – look in the fridge. Don't know when your father will be home, so don't wait dinner for him. And do go to bed early. You look tired.

Going straight from the game to the hospital had side-tracked Mike and he had no homework with him. Was he hungry? He should be. Worrying about the game had spoiled his appetite at lunch, and he'd had no real breakfast either, he remembered. He heated a frying pan and unwrapped one of the steaks. The smell as it hit the hot pan made his mouth water. He laid a single place at the kitchen table, filled a salad bowl and poured a glass of milk. Flipped the steak over.

He turned on the small TV above the kitchen counter – Mrs. Holden wouldn't work without a TV in the kitchen – and watched, not paying much attention, the antics of the Six Million Dollar Man. The steak was super, but halfway through he felt as if he couldn't eat another mouthful. He shovelled the remains guiltily into the garbage – too bad Mother said you shouldn't keep dogs in the city – rinsed his dishes and stacked them in the dishwasher.

In his own room, comfortably messy the way he liked it, he lifted the new rifle down from the rack above his desk and fingered it lovingly. The stock was of dark wood, smooth and silky with a curved comb. It fitted his shoulder and cheek exactly. He held it up to the window and sighted along the slim blued barrel.

He imagined a whitetail buck with an antler spread of sixty centimetres, with five long tines symmetrically placed, a North American trophy record. He raised the bolt handle and pulled back. Slid it forward and down, sighting through the scope. There was his deer seventy metres away, wonderful head raised, not yet alarmed but aware. Listening. He breathed in, aimed for the lung. Breathed out slowly, squeezing the trigger. Pow! A clean shot. The deer buckled at the knees and fell. Lay still with its great head on the snow....

Only a month to go. Twenty-six days to be exact. He pulled up the bolt and carefully wiped the rifle with an oily rag before restoring it to its rack. He snapped down the glass front and locked it. Put the key in the desk. Twenty-six whole days to go....

The sudden jangle of the phone made him nearly jump out of his skin. What was the matter with him anyway? He went to the kitchen extension.

"Hello?"

"Mike, how are you?" It was Gloria.

He let himself slide down to the floor until his back was resting comfortably against the fridge door. "Hi!"

"They told me – the guys on the team – that you had to go to the *hospital*. I was scared to death!"

Mike began to feel better. "Heck, nothing to worry about. Just flu, I guess."

"Are you feeling better now?"

"Sure. Great."

"Maybe we could go over to the Dairy Queen or something."

Mike swallowed a sudden nausea, remembering the steak he'd tossed into the garbage. "I ..."

"If you don't want to, that's okay."

"Gloria, you know I do. It's just, well, I really don't feel that great. I thought I'd go to bed early."

"Sure. Fine."

"I'm sorry."

"That's okay. See you around." The phone went dead.

Damn. He should have gone. But suppose he'd got sick or something? He sat with the phone in his hand, staring glumly at the tiled floor.

When he finally hung up it rang at once. He snatched it.

"Mike?"

"Oh, it's you, Doug."

"You want to try that again with more feeling?"

"Get off my case!"

"I called you before, but your line's been busy."

"Gloria phoned."

"So why d'you sound as if your pet goldfish just died?"

Mike snorted. "Oh, shut up."

"Sure." The phone went dead. Mike hung up and it instantly rang again. He picked it up. Doug went on talking. "So what's all this stuff about hospitals?"

"Nothing as far as I know." Mike told him about the doctor at Emergency. "... and you'd think that at least he'd prescribe an antibiotic or something. No kidding, I got the feeling that all he and old Alice were bothered about was making sure the school wasn't responsible."

"What d'you expect? It's the establishment. Anyway, how d'you feel now?"

"Tired."

"You better hit the sack."

"I was just going when you called."

"Sure you were. I've got X-ray vision. You were sitting staring at the phone and feeling pissed off. How come?"

"She wasn't too thrilled that I didn't feel up to going out this evening. Hey, I suppose you wouldn't feel like taking her to a movie or ... ?

"Not my style, thanks," Doug said hastily. "But heck, don't worry. She'll get over it. You're her blue-eyed boy, aren't you?"

Mike stared at the floor. "I made such an idiot of myself,"

he muttered. "I wish she hadn't been there."

"You mean fainting? Forget it. You know, when you went down I thought someone'd tripped you. I expect Gloria probably did too. Anyway it's over. You worry too much."

"Sure, grandpa."

"Well, someone's got to keep you straight, boy."

Mike chuckled and then yawned. "I'm bushed. See you tomorrow."

"You bet."

He couldn't help worrying that maybe there'd be some snide remarks about him making an ass of himself, not to mention helping lose the game – in spite of what Alice had said he still felt a bit guilty. But in fact nobody mentioned it at all the next day, except to say "Hi, hope you're feeling better."

He raced from class to class and spent lunch time and a spare in the library, doing the homework that should have been done the night before. He didn't even have a chance to talk to Gloria.

The phone was ringing its head off as he turned the key in the lock that afternoon. It stopped the second he got to it and all he heard was the dial tone. But it rang again half an hour later.

"Is Mrs. Rankin home?"

"No, I guess she's at some meeting or other. Is there a message?"

"Mr. Rankin?"

"No. Dad won't be back till late."

"That's Mike then?"

"Yes. Who ... ?"

"Dr. Hinton here. How are you feeling today?"

"Okay, I guess. A bit fluish still. How did you know ... oh, I suppose the hospital talked to you. You wanted to speak to Mother?"

"Yes, will you have her call me as soon as she gets in? Look, I'll give you my private number in case I've left the office by then – or have your father call, if he gets home first."

"He won't. He's got a late meeting."

"Well, have one of them call. Thanks." He gave the number and hung up abruptly.

Weird. Mike didn't know that there was anything wrong with Mother. Perhaps it was one of those female things like change of life. She looked all right. He scribbled a message, stuck it on the fridge door and went into his room to get on with the rest of his homework, taking a glass of milk and a couple of peanut butter sandwiches to hold him. Gun Club meeting at seven, and there'd be no time to finish his homework afterwards.

It was a good meeting. An hour's practice on the Boy Scouts' indoor range just down the block, then a short movie on still-hunting in the school library. There were only ten guys, all of them in grade twelve except for Doug and Mike and Laurie. Mr. Lee, the phys. ed. teacher, who was really into hunting, ran the discussion afterwards. The grade twelves did most of the talking, and Doug, of course. Nothing ever stopped Doug from talking. Mike mostly listened. You could learn a whole lot from listening.

They went along to Diamone's for pizza, and spent the next ten minutes arguing over the menu.

"Pick a number from one to twenty, then."

"Fifteen."

"Uh-uh. That's got shrimps. They give me hives. And anchovies."

"Okay then. Eighteen."

"Hawaiian."

"Yuck! Pineapple. That's gross."

"And no olives or peppers."

"Hey guys, that only leaves Three and Five. Pepperoni and cheese, or bacon and cheese."

"Okay. Hey Miss, we'll have a large Three and a large Five."

"You're new here, aren't you?" Doug made eyes at the girl and she giggled.

"What'll you all have to drink?"

"I'll have a Molson." Laurie spoke bass. "And one for my friends here."

The waitress looked at them suspiciously. Mr. Lee rescued her. "Cokes for these morons," he said firmly.

"Mr. Lee, that's not fair," Laurie protested. "I'll be eighteen in a couple of months."

The waitress went away and they bickered some more.

"I still don't understand why my score wasn't valid, Mr. Lee." John was an earnest-looking guy who'd just joined the club.

"Because you're only allowed two shots in each of five targets," Mr. Lee explained patiently for the second time.

"And you had four or five shots in each of yours."

"But I only fired off ten shots." John looked around for support. "Honest."

"Something's rotten in wherever," Rick said. "It was one of you grade eleven wimps, that's what."

"Us?" Doug looked around in astonishment. Mike tried to keep his face blank, but he wasn't a patch on Doug. They'd shot off their rounds early and had some fun with the new guy while he'd still been sighting on his first target.

"I'm sure it won't happen again, John. Will it, guys?"

Doug and Mike stared innocently back.

"I'm confused about still-hunting and hunting from a stand," John said awkwardly. He knew he was being roasted, but wasn't sure how.

Doug laughed. "Still-hunting is Mike's specialty, isn't it, Mike? It sure worked with Gloria. You just stayed quiet and let her catch you."

"Hey Doug, stick it, will you!" Mike flushed and kicked Doug under the table. The others roared.

Mr. Diamone came over to their booth. "Excuse me." He tried to make himself heard above the laughter.

"Sorry, are we making too much noise?" Mr. Lee apologized.

"Oh no, no. That's all right. But is Mike Rankin here?"

"Sure, that's me. Why?"

Mr. Diamone grinned knowingly, a wide smile with gold in its corners. "Your Momma phoned here twice. She wants you to go home right now!"

The grade twelve guys catcalled.

"Poor baby!" Steve crooned.

"Late again, naughty boy!" Rick said in falsetto.

"Come on, shut up!" Mike spluttered. He could feel his face turn red again. He glanced at the clock. Only just after nine-thirty. He stuck out his chin. "I'll eat first."

"That's telling them," Laurie approved.

Doug kicked him under the table. "Why don't you phone?" he whispered. "I mean, it's not really like your mother, is it?"

"No, it's not. But gee, in front of these guys ..." He fished in his jeans pocket. "Damn, have you got a dime?"

"Sure. Take it easy, Mike."

The phone rang only twice before he heard his mother's voice.

"It's me, Mom."

"Oh, thank goodness, Mike."

"Mom, what's up? Is something wrong with Dad?" He felt a sudden tightness like a band of metal around his chest. He couldn't breathe and had to lean against the tile wall next to the phone.

"Why, no. Did you think ... ? I'm so sorry. It's just that we have to talk. Will you come home now, dear?"

He took a deep breath as the panic subsided. "*Now?* Mom, it's only nine-thirty, and we've just ordered." There was silence at the other end. "Mom, are you still there?"

"Yes." Her voice sounded brisk. "I'm sorry. I wasn't thinking. Look, finish your pizza, and then come right home, all right?"

"Sure. Mom...."

"Yes, dear?"

"You're sure you're okay? I mean, of course I'll come right now if ..."

"No, no. I didn't mean to scare you. We're both fine. See you soon."

Mike put down the phone and went back to the booth.

"Off the hook, eh?" Rick teased.

"Sure. No sweat. I told her to quit bugging me. You know mothers." Right after saying it, Mike wished he hadn't. Sometimes it was hard to go on being loyal and yet get in with the right crowd.

The pizzas arrived just then. As they reached for pieces Doug whispered, "Everything okay?"

"Sure. I think so."

Mike wasn't really hungry. He ate a token piece of pizza and finished his Coke. "Well, I'm off. See you guys." He put three dollars on the table. "Look after mine, will you, Doug?"

It had turned cold all of a sudden and the sky was overcast and leaden looking. There'd be a skiff of snow before long. Perfect hunting weather. He shoved his hands into the pockets of his jacket. It was Hallowe'en. The streets were almost empty now, but there were still a few lit pumpkins out on porches. Tomorrow would be November 1st. Not long to wait now....

He walked fast, bothered by Mother's phone call. It wasn't like her to fuss. She'd said there was nothing wrong with her or Dad, but ... Dr. Hinton had called. And there were stories in the paper every day of business men in their forties having heart attacks. Dad was almost fifty. Suppose ...

By the time Mike had turned down the crescent that led to his house he was almost running and horribly out of breath. He had to lean against a lamp post and get a second wind for the last haul up the hill.

They were waiting for him in the living room. Some time earlier a fire had been lit, but they'd let it die down, or forgotten it maybe, so that now it was nothing but ashes and a faint glow. They both looked up, smiled, moved, said hello as he came in; but he had the odd feeling that before he'd come in they'd just been sitting like statues staring at that dead fire.

Dad looked fine. Mike sat down suddenly on the nearest chair as his knees went soft. Mom looked okay too. He took in a deep, thankful breath.

"So what's with you two? You scared the hell out of me."

"I'm sorry, dear. Sometimes you stay out late and we wanted to talk tonight. I think I panicked a little."

"It's all right, Mom." He looked enquiringly from one to the other. The last piece of log in the fireplace collapsed with a soft sound and a shower of sparks.

Mother undamped her hands and held them out automatically to the non-existent flames. "Dr. Hinton called today, Mike. He got the report from the doctor who examined you in Emergency yesterday. It seems that your tiredness and that fainting spell weren't just flu. You're very anaemic. It could be mono or ..."

"Or something a bit more complicated," Dad went on as

Mother faltered. "Anyway they want to have you admitted to the hospital for a couple of days to run some tests."

"Hospital? Me?" Mike looked at them blankly. He'd always been so healthy. No tonsils or appendix. Only Emergency a few times to stitch up cuts ...

"Oh, it won't be so bad, Mike. And the rest'll do you good."

"Are you sure Dr. Hinton's not fussing about nothing? Honestly, I just feel a bit dragged down. And there is a lot of flu about."

"Maybe that's it." Mother stopped warming her hands at the dead fire and smiled at him. She looked tired. "Dr. Hinton is a bit of an old fuddy-duddy. That's the price you pay for a family doctor who's known your parents most of their lives, *and* delivered you into the bargain."

"And the tests will at least prove that there's nothing to worry about. Remember that time two years ago when I got those awful chest pains, Anita? Boy, we really thought it was game over. But it turned out to be nothing worse than tension."

"I suppose the worst that'll happen will be mono. Gloria will kill me and I'll have to take it easy for ages. Boring."

"That'll be it." Dad got to his feet and put a hand on Mike's shoulder. "Off you go, son, and get a good night's sleep. I've promised to deliver you to Admitting before nine tomorrow morning. You'll have to pack a bag."

"Shall I do it for you, dear?"

"No, that's all right, Mom. What should I take?"

"Oh, toothbrush. Pyjamas. Bathrobe and slippers. It's

only for a couple of days."

"And you'd better slip in a paperback and some of those word-search games of yours. My memory of lab tests is hours and hours of waiting around. You'll probably be bored out of your tree!"

THREE

Dad was right. Once Mike had hurdled the uncomfortable strangeness of Admitting and had climbed into a high cold bed in the middle of the day, there were four blank walls and a television with nothing to see but game shows and kindergarten programs. There was absolutely nothing to do but sit there feeling bored and wait for the door to swing open and admit yet another technician with a covered tray, syringes and dozens of little glass containers.

"I don't need a private room," he had objected as they had gone through Admitting, but the wave of Dad's hand said clearly: only the best is good enough for George Rankin's son. He didn't seem to hear what Mike was saying. It had all been arranged. Mike sighed. If he were in a ward there would at least be someone to talk to. He riffled through the latest Len Deighton, but even spies couldn't hold his attention.

After a very long morning he heard the rattle of lunch trays. That cheered him up. But nobody came in, and after a while the noise died away and an afternoon sleepiness seemed to envelop the corridor outside. Mike's stomach rumbled noisily. Had they forgotten him? He wondered if he should ring, but didn't have the nerve – suppose they thought it was an emergency?

The door swung open at last. About time! But it was only a male attendant with a wheelchair.

"Hey, whatabout my lunch?"

"I wouldn't know about that. I'm just supposed to take you along to the treatment room."

"What for?"

"Sorry. I wouldn't know that either."

He felt ridiculous in a wheelchair, especially since they only went along the corridor, across a wide hall with easy chairs and elevators, and down another corridor, ending up in a small white cubicle like the inside of an empty refrigerator, with the words "Treatment Room Four" on the door.

Treatment? The attendant and the chair vanished, leaving Mike sitting in his dressing gown on the room's only chair. Everything that was not made of polished steel seemed to be made of white tile. No sound penetrated from beyond the closed door. It was extraordinarily cold. Mike found himself shivering. Not that he was scared or anything. But this room ...

The door opened to admit a doctor and a nurse, neither of whom he had seen before.

"Hello...." The doctor glanced at the clipboard in his hand. "Hello, Michael. I'm Doctor Wagner, one of the residents. I expect you're beginning to wonder what's been going on all day."

"Yes. Especially what happened to lunch. Why ... ?"

"Just be patient a little longer." It seemed that he hadn't really been listening either. "One more procedure. We'll have you on the table, please, on your back. No dressing gown or pyjama top."

Mike lay back, feeling steadily hungrier and colder, and he nearly yelled out loud when the nurse slathered his chest with something wet and icy.

She grinned sympathetically at his expression. "Only antiseptic," she told him softly. "I'm sorry about your lunch. Someone should have explained. This procedure is better done on an empty stomach."

He would have liked to ask her what was going on, but he didn't feel he could with the square-jawed resident standing by. His chest felt numb, and he looked down in surprise. "Hey, what's going on? You're not operating on me, are you? There's nothing wrong with my chest..."

"Take it easy. We are just testing the healthiness of your blood supply. You may get a bit of pain in your sternum, but it will only be momentary. Just shut your eyes and relax."

Mike shut his eyes, but too late. He caught a glimpse of the most enormous syringe and needle, more like something for breaking up roads than for people. He screwed his eyes shut and held his breath.

"Just breathe regularly and try to relax," the calm voice went on. *Relax?* A sudden pain caught him by surprise in the dead centre of his chest. He gasped.

"Steady," came the voice, remote, preoccupied.

Somebody was holding his hand. Soft and warm. He hung on and felt the hand squeeze back. She was all right, this nurse. A terrific chick in fact. He could feel the sweat running down his face. The room suddenly dipped and circled and he was glad that he hadn't been given any lunch. He gulped.

The pain stopped, to be replaced by a dull ache. He was almost grateful for it. He felt the pressure of a dressing against his chest. He cautiously opened his eyes. The nurse let go of his hand and fetched a damp cloth to wipe his face and shoulders. He was sweating as if he'd just finished a basketball game.

"Lie still until the attendant comes to take you back to your room." Square jaws flashed a brief mechanical smile and left with a tray covered with a white cloth. The nurse helped Mike into his pyjama top and dressing gown. He was happy just to lie back afterwards on the hard table and watch her tidy the room. She gave him a warm smile before she went out. Pretty. And gorgeous legs.

More technicians came in during the afternoon. They took more blood. They took swabs of his nose and throat and ears. He was peered at from hair to toe nails. After a while he slid down under the white covers and pretended to be asleep. Not that it did any good.

"When do I get to leave? What's wrong anyway?" he asked every time someone came in, but all he got were polite evasions or blank looks. Then Dr. Hinton strolled in, looking unofficial in grey slacks and a navy blazer. Mike repeated his questions.

"You have quite a severe anaemia," Dr. Hinton told him. "Tomorrow morning you'll get a special kind of transfusion, and then we'll start treatment. I'm afraid you'll have to take life fairly easy for a while, no marathons – oh, it's basketball, isn't it? But once we've got you stabilized you'll be able to go home and just come in on weekends for treatment."

"Weekends? For how long?"

"Oh, it's too hard to tell at this stage."

"I've got to be better by the weekend of the 27th."

"Of November? Well, I can't promise, but you should be feeling pretty good by then. What's the special event? A school dance?"

"Uh-uh. Four days off school. And the end of the hunting season. We're off to Swan Hills to bag a couple of deer."

Dr. Hinton frowned. "Your father didn't mention any trips."

"I guess he forgot. He's not into that sort of thing. Though you should see the super rifle he got me for my birthday! No, I'm going with Doug O'Reilly and his dad."

"Been planning it long?" Dr. Hinton sat on the end of the bed and swung his glasses by one ear-piece.

"You'd better believe it. All *year!* This is the first fall either of us has been old enough to buy a Big Game licence."

Dr. Hinton shook his head slowly. "I hate to disappoint you, Mike, but it's out of the question."

"What d'you mean? I have to be fit by then. You just said I'd be fine."

"I said you should be feeling fine. It's not quite the same thing."

"Near enough. No stupid anaemia is going to stop me going on that hunting trip."

Dr. Hinton got off the bed. He looked down at Mike. For a minute he looked as if he were going to go on arguing. Then he just shrugged. "Well, I'll leave that up to George and Anita. You can argue it out with them when you see them this evening."

———

It was Doug who arrived first, soon after a depressing supper of cream of potato soup, white fish in some kind of guck, and rice pudding. Mike found himself thinking regretfully about the steak he'd tossed in the garbage a couple of days before.

Doug bounced into the room, all freckles and red hair, somehow extra large and healthy in the small room. "Hey, Mike, how're you feeling?"

"Okay, I guess. At least if they'd stop sticking needles into me. You wouldn't believe the one this afternoon..." He made a good story of it, only exaggerating a little, describing the gorgeous nurse and how he'd got her to hold his hand.

Doug chuckled and sat down heavily on Mike's feet. "Boy, you'd better not let Gloria hear that."

"Are you kidding? Er ... did you see her around today?" he went on casually.

"Yeah, she was in the Dive at lunch time," Doug answered even more casually. Then he grinned and went on. "She was asking how you were, whether you'd be home soon, that kind of stuff...."

"She was?" Mike beamed.

"I said I'd let her know when you were getting sprung. D'you know?"

"They haven't said. They don't say *anything*," Mike exploded

"Haven't they said what's wrong?"

Mike shook his head. "Some kind of anaemia. They've taken so much blood already I feel like a vampire victim, I'm probably anaemic now even if I wasn't before."

"Gee, you'll be okay for our trip, won't you?"

"You bet I will. Nothing, but absolutely nothing's going to get in the way of that!"

"Get in the way of what, Mike?" Mother came smiling into the room, Dad right behind her. "Why, hello, Doug, nice to see you."

"Hi, Mrs. Rankin. Mr. Rankin." Doug scrambled off the bed.

"We were talking about our trip up to Swan Hills, Mom. At the end of next month. Hey, no, today's the first of November, isn't it? The end of this month. When I get to try out that new Weatherby, Dad."

"What? Oh, your gun. Yes, I'd forgotten all about that."

"Well I sure haven't. And neither's Doug. It's going to be a fantastic long weekend."

Mother looked meaningfully at Dad. She was paler than usual, Mike thought. Maybe it was the hospital atmosphere. It seemed to make both of them a little tense.

Dad broke the silence. "Look, son. I think you're going to have to face the possibility of missing that trip north...."

"Hey, no way!"

"Since Dr. Hinton feels that it wouldn't be wise ..."

"You said yourself he was a fuss-pot, Mom. You know he overreacts."

"Nevertheless, Mike ..."

"Mrs. Rankin, we'd look out for Mike, Dad and me. We wouldn't let him overdo it. Four days in the bush is no big deal, honest."

Mother looked blankly at Doug, almost as if she wasn't really seeing him at all. Doug turned red from his neck right up to his forehead, but he didn't give up. "I promise we'll look after him."

Mother seemed to pull herself together. She put a hand on Doug's arm. "Thank you, Doug. That's good of you. I know you want what's best for Mike. And so do we. You must realize that."

"Hey, what about me?" Mike interrupted. "Don't I have a say?"

"We're going to have to abide by the doctor's decision," Mother went on as if she hadn't heard him. "Now, Doug, I wonder if you'd mind ..." She paused and looked at the door, and Doug caught on.

"Oh, sure. Goodnight, Mrs. Rankin. Goodnight, sir. Bye, Mike. See you later."

"Hey, no! Look, Doug, wait up."

"Thank you for coming, Doug." Dad closed the door.

"Shit, why did you do that!" Mike was nearly in tears.

"Mike! Don't use that kind of language in front of your mother."

"Sorry, Mom," Mike muttered. "But you know I wanted him to stay. He only just got here and he hadn't finished telling me about Gloria and ... and everything," he finished lamely.

Mother smiled tiredly. She ran a hand through her hair in a very uncharacteristic way that mussed up her perfect set. "Oh, Mike, we want a chance to talk to you too. You'll see lots of Doug later. My goodness, you've only been gone a day and already I'm missing you."

"I've missed you too," Mike said dutifully. "And home-cooking. The food here – yuck!" He made an effort to be cheerful.

Dad joined in. "I remember the worst thing about my stay in the hospital was the food. Everything white and wet. And the boredom! Do you need any more books, son?"

"I sure hope not! How long am I going to be in here any-way? Nobody's told me *anything*."

There was a hesitation. Or did he imagine it? Maybe this place was getting on his nerves too.

"Dr. Hinton thought you might have to stay just a few more days. Try and be patient, dear."

"I don't mean to be a drag, Mom, but it's not knowing what's going on that gets to me."

"Well, it won't be long before you're home, I'm sure. And you know what I've been thinking? I spend entirely too much of my time on committees, running around the city. I'd like to spend more time at home with you."

"Hey, that's great. But ... I mean, don't do anything rash

after all, I'm in school most of the time anyway." He frowned. "I hope I don't get too far behind. I hate trying to follow other people's notes."

"Don't worry about it, son. After all, there's no real need to sweat till grade twelve, till you're thinking about university." Dad stood stiffly at the foot of the bed. Funny how different people react to different settings, Mike thought. How would Gloria be, he wondered, and imagined her sitting beside him, maybe holding his hand.

"I think he's tired, Anita."

"Yes. We'd better let you get a good night's sleep." Mother kissed his cheek and Dad patted his shoulder. Then the door swung shut behind them, leaving an unsettled air, like the feeling in an airport terminal.

He was wide awake and bored, bored. He flipped the TV control from channel to channel. They all seemed equally stupid. He picked up the Len Deighton he'd been reading, and threw it down again after a few pages. He couldn't even keep track of the characters' names. Nothing to do. Just watch the clock above the door. And worry ...

Ta-tatatata-taTAH. A very unprofessional-sounding knock at the door. He sat up. "Come in!"

Doug's curly red head poked around the edge of the door. "All clear? Or are they coming back?"

"No, they've gone home. I thought you'd gone. Glad to see you, shit-head."

"Well, I realized I couldn't get a bus home for over half an hour, so I stopped for a Coke. Then I saw your parents in the lobby, so I nipped up again and sneaked past the desk. What's up, Mike?"

"What d'you mean?"

"They looked awfully upset."

"They did?"

"Maybe I'm imagining it. Forget it. It's this spooky place. Gets to you after a while. I know. I had my tonsils out here. Never felt so down in my life. I thought Mom and Dad had left me for good, and I couldn't figure out what I'd done that was so awful."

"You're putting me on."

"Uh-uh. Honest to God."

"Hmm. How old were you anyway?"

"Four."

"You jerk!" Mike laughed, and then felt depressed again. "Hey, I'm kind of worried about that trip. Suppose I can't make it. Suppose they really won't let me."

"It's almost a month away. No reason why things shouldn't be cool by then. Don't borrow trouble, Mike."

"I know. But ..."

"Look, just concentrate on getting better. You know, mind over matter. Then you can get the doctor to say you're fit, and there'll be no more trouble. Right?"

"I suppose." Mike kicked miserably at the bedclothes. "Oh, get off my feet. You weigh a ton and I'm getting pins and needles."

"Hey, if worst comes to worst, there's always next year."

"Next year! Shit, Doug, I couldn't wait a whole year."

"Well, that's the worst that could happen. Probably you're fussing about nothing as usual. Wait and see how it goes."

"And no basketball. I'll never get back on the senior team," Mike added gloomily.

"Quit complaining. Think about missing social studies. And math! Hey, wait till I tell you the boner Mrs. Morgan pulled in Assembly today. Everybody wet themselves laughing and she blushed for the rest of the day."

Doug began to spin one of his long-drawn-out yarns and soon Mike was laughing hard enough to attract the attention of a passing nurse. "What are you doing in here? I thought I saw you leave earlier," she said to Doug.

"I just slipped down for a drink."

"I'm not sure that Michael is supposed to have any visitors."

"Oh, come on, nurse. Please."

"Well, there's only five minutes left anyway. I suppose it won't hurt. But keep the noise down, will you?"

"You'll come back tomorrow, won't you?" Mike asked in a sudden panic, after she'd gone. "I ... you know ... well, it's as boring as hell in here."

"Sure, I'll come. Any time." They punched each other amicably and in a couple of minutes the buzzer went and Mike was alone again.

Next morning there was a new face. A new doctor. By now Mike was beginning to feel like a weekend roast going through a supermarket assembly line. But this man was different. For starters he came over to the bed and introduced himself properly. "I'm Dr. Gage. Jim Gage. Do you prefer Mike or Michael?"

"Er, Mike, thanks." He shook the proffered hand. "What's happened to Dr. Hinton?"

"Oh, I'm sure he'll drop in for a chat now and then, keep an eye on you. But he's a general practitioner, and since I'm a specialist in diseases of the blood I'm going to take over your case."

Uh. Mike was taken aback. A *specialist*? Dr. Gage seemed kind of young-looking to be a specialist in anything, he thought, with his smooth pinky skin that looked as if it never needed shaving. But it was a pleasant face and his greenish hazel eyes looked frank, as if he was the sort of person you could ask questions. "I feel pretty stupid in here," he ventured. "You know, I'm really only a bit tired ..."

"Short of breath?"

"Sometimes. Just when I run. Not now."

"That's the anaemia. We're going to give you a special kind of transfusion that'll make you feel like a million dollars."

"Then I can go home?"

"Whoa. Not quite so fast! Look, don't feel guilty about being here. If we felt you didn't need the bed we'd toss you out fast enough, believe me. After the transfusion we'll start you on treatment. We'll have to watch and see how you react to it. There are pills. You'll be taking them four times a day for at least four weeks. Then we'll see how you're progressing. There are a few side effects, nothing too troublesome. You might put on a bit of weight, but you look as if you could stand a few extra kilos, eh?" The doctor sat on the edge of the bed, and Mike couldn't help grinning, thinking how guilty Doug had looked when Mother had caught him doing just that.

"So once I'm on these pills I can go back to school?"

"I hope so."

"And go camping on the last weekend in November?"

"Hang on a minute. You're jumping ahead of me. The bad news is the second medication. It has to be given intravenously, so you have to come into the hospital for that."

"But you just said I'd be able to go back to school."

"Yes. The IV will be only once a week. You'll be able to come in on Saturdays."

"But ..."

"You see the problem is that the drug that is most effective in dealing with your particular problem is also very toxic. That means that it must be administered very carefully, and we have to keep an eye on you, look out for adverse effects."

"So if I'm taking this stuff I can't go hunting, that's what you're saying?"

"Yes. I'm really sorry."

"Okay. So we don't start the treatment till December. After all, that's less than a month away, and as you said, the transfusion will make me feel good as new...." Mike stopped talking. The doctor was shaking his head. "You can't *make* me take any treatment." He stuck out his jaw.

Dr. Gage just looked at Mike with serious, steady eyes and didn't say anything for a minute. Mike swallowed.

"Look, fella." The doctor spoke quietly. "I'd hate to have to work with you under those conditions, but the fact of the matter is that your parents *did* admit you here, and they *did* sign the consent form for this treatment. I'm sorry, Mike, but you are under age. That's a fact. But I'd certainly rather work with your co-operation."

"The intravenous stuff ... what's it called?"

"Vincristine."

"Couldn't you leave it for a bit? Just give me the pills." Again Dr. Gage shook his head. Mike felt angry and helpless and sudden tears sprang into his eyes. Damn. In a minute he'd start bawling in front of this total stranger.

Dr. Gage got off the bed. He didn't seem to have noticed that anything was wrong. "Why don't I drop by and talk to you later? I really should get on with my round or the head nurse will have my neck."

He went out, shutting the door behind him so that mercifully Mike was alone. He sat up in bed with his knees hunched up and his forehead leaning on them. Everything had been going so well. It had seemed as if high school was going to be a great and golden time. Now all of a sudden he'd lost control of his life. As if something he'd been holding had unexpectedly turned into water and slid between his fingers.

After a while he blew his nose, got up and went into the tiny bathroom and washed his face. He was standing by the window, staring absentmindedly at the activity in the parking lot below, when Dr. Gage returned a couple of hours later.

Mike managed a small tight grin. "Well, let's get started with this dumb treatment then. Somehow I'm going to make that trip."

—

If he had been able to look ahead at that moment, what would he have done? Was hope enough? Or would he have run from it all, as he was running now....

In memory the bad days and moments ran together, though in real time, when he thought about it, they must have been separated by weeks in which everybody conspired to pretend that life was perfectly normal.

—

There was the pain. They never told him how much the stuff would hurt. And then, in spite of anti-nausea drugs, there were spells of uncontrollable, exhausting vomiting. He'd recover from that and go back to school, and on the surface everything would be just as it had been before. But it wasn't, not really.

"Mike, what's the matter? You haven't said a word all evening," Gloria accused him over a pizza, after an early movie one Friday night in mid-November. It had to be the early show so he'd be rested up for his Saturday appointment at the hospital. It affects everything, he thought gloomily. Grade eleven and I have to go to the early show.

"Mike!"

"Huh?"

"If you can't even pay attention when I talk to you I'm going home. Mike, you're no fun any more."

"Hey, I'm sorry. Really. Please don't go. You know how important you are to me, how ..." Mike stopped. He was afraid of getting too intense, of scaring her off by letting her know that it was only thinking about her that kept him going when the treatment got too bad. "It's just ..." He hesitated. "On Monday and Tuesday I'm just getting over this dumb treatment. Then the rest of the week I'm dreading Saturday again."

Gloria sighed. "How long do you think it'll go on for?" She pushed her heavy dark hair back from her neck. He longed to reach out and touch it, bury his face in it. He took a long drag of milkshake.

"I don't know. I've asked Dr. Gage and Dr. Hinton. I've even asked Mother and Dad to ask them. But nobody'll tell me anything. 'Soon.' 'Be patient, dear.' 'A couple more weeks and you'll be as good as new,'" he mimicked, and stirred his milkshake moodily. "I don't trust them any more.... Not the parents or the doctors."

Gloria sucked up the last of her drink and wiped her fingers carefully. "Mike, I want to go home. This evening's a drag."

"Gloria, please."

"*Now*, Mike."

After that he was extra careful to hide his feelings, but having to pretend made life even more unreal than it was already.

The worst of the nightmare came one morning at home

when the alarm went off and he stumbled half asleep into the bathroom. He was staring blankly at the mirror on the medicine cabinet when he saw the bare patch on the left side of his head, where he'd slept. Bare scalp. Skin! He could still remember staring, blinking and staring again. In a panic he ran back into the bedroom, not believing it, to see the tufts of hair grotesquely strewn on his pillow.

Somehow he managed to call Dr. Gage at the hospital, failed to find him there, called his private number. He was still on the line listening to the phone ring, his heart bumping against his chest, when Mother came out of the kitchen, whisk in one hand, eggs in the other. He saw the eggs fall to the tiled floor, smashing and spreading glutinously.

He looked from the mess to her face. She hadn't even noticed the eggs. She was staring at his head with a strange expression of horror and ... disgust? Then her face changed. "Oh, my poor baby!" and she moved towards him.

Dr. Gage was finally on the phone. He could hear his voice. "Hello! Hello! Who's there?"

"You bastard," he said into the phone. "Why didn't you tell me?" And he slammed the receiver down and ran to his room to hide from the expression on Mother's face.

He locked the door and lay face down on the bed for a long time. His heart beat so hard it seemed to shake his whole body. What was happening to him? Was he falling apart, some disease so ugly they wouldn't tell him? Like leprosy. Oh, God, stop it, whatever it is! He tried to fight the panic. He was cold all over and shivering.

After a while he started thinking about Mother and Dad. Did they know this would happen? What else were they hiding from him? Then he thought about Dr. Gage. He'd really trusted him. What was with adults anyway? He began to get angry, and the anger took away the shakes.

Later he got up off the bed and made himself walk across the room and look at the reflection in the mirror. Was it all going to fall out? He took up his hair brush and brushed it savagely, until his scalp stung. He looked at the brush, wadded with hair, and let it fall to the floor.

Then he stared at himself, as one might look at a stranger in a bus depot. His remaining hair hung in fair tufts with bare patches between. He looked as if he'd got some foul kind of skin disease. His face was a bit puffy from the medicine and it seemed to him to bear no relationship to the face he was used to, the face he'd grown up with. Yet inside he was still the Mike he knew.

But other people didn't know that. They'd only know what they saw. He couldn't let anyone see him like this ... let Gloria? He'd die a slow and agonizing death before he'd ever let Gloria see him looking like this.

He wandered aimlessly around the room, still a bit shivery. Then he made up his mind. He got out his nail scissors and carefully cut off all the remaining locks of hair. His hands weren't too steady and it took ages. When he was through his scalp was a mixture of white baldness and uneven stubble. Horrible. Almost worse, if anything could be. He took the new razor that Mother had given him for his birthday and carefully went over his entire head. The bits at the back were difficult, and his skull was much more knobby than he had expected, but at last the job was done.

As he switched off the razor he became aware of an insistent knocking at the bedroom door. "Mike! Mike, please talk to me. What are you doing in there?"

"Nothing, Mother." He cleaned the razor meticulously and put it away in its case. He cleaned up the tufts of hair that lay on the bedroom floor and threw them into the waste basket and he shook over the basket the tufts that still clung to his pillow case.

"Son."

It was Dad's voice. What was he doing home at this time of the day? He looked at the clock. Noon. It had been early morning when he had woken up and first looked in the mirror. What had happened to the rest of the morning?

"What do you want?" His voice was quite steady. His hands had become steady too, all the time that he'd been shaving his head.

"I want to explain about your hair. Don't be upset. It's only a side effect of the medicine. Dr. Gage told us about it."

"And you didn't tell me? What's with you anyway? Didn't you think it might be a bit of a shock to wake up and find half my hair lying on the pillow, for God's sake?"

"I'm sorry." It was Mother. Her voice was choked up, as if she'd been crying. He ought to be upset, but all he felt was savagely angry. "I'm sorry, Mikey," she went on, calling him the baby name she hadn't used in years. "Dr. Gage wanted to tell you, but we wouldn't let him. I thought maybe it won't happen and why should you be worried."

Mike looked at the stranger in the mirror, puffy-faced and bald as a cue-ball, and began to laugh. "You didn't want me to *worry*. Oh, Mother, that's rich. That's really rich,"

"I thought it would just get a little thin. I thought we could tell you if that began to happen. I didn't know it was going to happen all at once like ... like ..."

"Like this?" He unlocked the bedroom door and yanked it open.

Mother's hands went to her mouth. "You've shaved it off. Your lovely blond hair. Oh, Mike."

"I'd rather have none than patches. Cheer up, Mother, maybe it'll grow on you. Get it? *Grow* on you."

Dad made a great effort and rallied. "At least you won't waste so much money getting it styled, or all that time in the mornings messing around with blow dryers and all that nonsense."

"Sure, Dad, you've got it. Think of all the time I'll save And who knows, maybe it'll wow the girls. If it's good enough for Kojak..." His lips trembled, so that it was hard to go on grinning. He thought of Gloria, saw her face in some strange way superimposed on Mother's. He remembered Mother's face when she'd first seen him. His shoulders sagged and the grin vanished. He suddenly felt sick. "I can't go to school."

"What do you mean? Darling, do you feel ill?"

"I won't go to school. Not like this. Uh-uh. No way!"

"Come on, son. I'm sure your friends will be too mannerly to mention it."

"Can't you see that'd be worse? Everyone staring. Or trying not to stare. And Gloria ... all the girls ... no, I can't. No way."

"Oh, George, I know how he feels. Maybe he *should* stay home if he wants to. Just till it grows back. It will, won't it?"

"As soon as Mike's off that medication. Dr. Gage told us that. But he also said Mike should lead as normal a life as possible. That includes school."

"Normal?" Mike began to laugh. "You call the way I look normal? I'm not going and that's it. Either I stay home or I stop the treatment. One or the other."

For a couple of weeks he hid in the house, except for hospital visits, and wouldn't see anyone, even Doug. He played endless games of cribbage with Mother, and watched all the stupid daytime shows on TV. At the end of two weeks he was bored out of his tree.

Then Doug came over one Saturday and Mother let him in, and there was Mike, caught in the living room. Doug took one look at him and roared with laughter. He laughed until he had to hold onto a chair.

Mike found he was smiling too. "Shit, you bastard. Stop it!"

"It's so pale. Must be from hiding under your pillow all day," Doug gasped between laughs.

"What the hell do you mean by that?"

"Well, isn't that where you've been?"

They stared at each other, Mike suddenly flushed with anger, Doug's eyes level.

"It's not like that," Mike stammered.

"Like what?"

"Like you said – hiding."

"Could have fooled me."

"It's just ... jeez, Doug, what'll everyone say?"

"I don't know. It's funny as hell when you first see it. So what? It's only hair. Or not, in this case. I expect they'll just laugh and forget about it."

"I don't think I can handle that."

"Sure you can. Get a cap. A jazzy ski toque."

"D'you think I could?"

"Sure. After a week or so people won't even notice."

"The girls ..." His voice faded.

"You mean Gloria, don't you? Look, Mike, you might as well know now as later. Since you've stayed home she's been going out pretty steadily with a guy in grade twelve."

"Yeah?"

"Yeah."

Mike stared at the living-room carpet as if he was trying to memorize the design. Then he stood up. "Let's go over to Woodward's and pick up a toque. Something with real class."

Doug was right. People stared at first. Sometimes a kid would say, "Why are you wearing that dumb cap in school?" and then *he'd* say, "To keep my head warm, stupid," and pull it off. It was good for a laugh every time. And it didn't matter, because he'd made the laughter happen.

Things were okay. Except for Gloria. The first day she saw him she gave him a small careful smile, as if her face might crack. "Hi, Mike."

"Hi, Gloria, how've you been?"

"Fine, thanks." Over her shoulder, as she kept walking, as if she were afraid she'd catch whatever it was.

Sometimes at night when he couldn't get to sleep he'd lie awake and dream up scenarios in which she loved him and the baldness didn't matter at all – in fact she found it sexy. And he'd dream of doing all sorts of impossible things to make her admire him even more.

But those were kid daydreams. The truth came in his nightmares, when he heard, for the millionth time in his mind, the awful things he'd overheard her say about him – things he couldn't let his waking mind remember.

After that he wouldn't let himself daydream about her any more. But the nightmares still came back....

FOUR

Something woke him. Something loud and close and sudden. He lay and listened to his heart hammering in the silence and for a moment he couldn't remember where he was. In his own room at home? In the hospital? He could see nothing at all, but when he moved he felt the squeak of the air mattress under him. A draft of intensely cold air rushed down the opening at the top of the sleeping bag. Then he remembered.

Inside the tent the darkness was almost solid, like mud, and it seemed to be pressing in on him from every side. He had the crazy feeling that even to breathe might be dangerous, that he might suffocate if he drew this blackness down into his lungs.

He lay rigid in his sleeping bag and stared at the dark as one might stare at an enemy, waiting for it to make the first move. After a long time it seemed to him that he was winning. The darkness moved reluctantly back, not far, but far enough for him to see a small triangle of dimness. The tent door. The forest. And the night sky.

Quickly, before the enemy could catch him, he wriggled out of the sleeping bag and scudded across the tent floor on hands and knees. Just outside was his friend, the fire. Had it gone out? When he was close enough he could see a faint pink glow hidden in the heart of a charcoal log.

He knelt on the frozen grass and blew frantically. Blew off a cloud of fine ash and sparks. The wood glowed rosily and then faded with each puff of air. It was as if he were breathing new life into the wood. In and out. In and out. He found twigs, dry moss, grass. Tucked them around the living wood and blew again. A yellow flame licked out, wrapped itself around the log, flared through the grass. He laid newly cut wood across the top, being careful not to bury the small flames under too much weight.

The flames rose high and the darkness moved back reluctantly almost to the circle of trees. He had left the pot of water close to the fire before he had gone to bed, and now he set it right over the flames and tipped instant coffee and sugar into his mug.

It took some time to boil, and while he was waiting he shrugged into his downfill and then stood up and stretched and stared at the sky. The pattern of constellations had moved since he had gone to bed, but the awful emptiness beyond and between the stars had not changed. God, how empty space was! On and on forever. Was eternity going to be like that? Was that what was waiting for him out there?

The water boiled and he filled the mug with hands that shook a little, just with the cold, he told himself. He squatted in the entrance of the tent with the glow of the flames reflecting comfortably off his front and the coffee mug clasped between his hands.

A long wavering howl shivered through the dark trees. It was echoed by another. And another. The silence between the howls was like the dark beyond the fire, but more fearful, more intense. He scurried back into the warmth of his sleeping bag, lay on his stomach, the coffee mug between his hands, while the cold howls surrounded him with their sorrow.

"A coyote's voice will travel incredibly far." Doug's father's voice came to him as if he were right there in the tent. "You'll swear they're right around your camp, but actually they could be a couple of valleys away. They're shy beasts. You'll hear them, but you'll rarely get a glimpse of them."

Mike sipped his coffee. It was hot and sweet and smoky. The gunshot cry of a tree in the grip of the frost echoed through the silence and he knew what it was that had awakened him.

When the coffee was finished down to the last sugary drop he wriggled down into the sleeping bag until only his forehead, nose and eyes were exposed. The tent was now a cosy cave flooded with flickering rose-gold. Through the triangle of the door the light of the fire defined the pile of logs, the boulder behind, the saucepan, comfortably domestic, set to one side.

Beyond that there was a nothingness that was now filled with sounds. Had they been there before? Or had his ears just developed a new sensitivity because all the ordinary sounds he filled them with – the radio, the TV – all these distractions were gone? He heard several kinds of small rustlings. A patter among dry leaves. A miniscule thud. There was nothing frightening about these noises. He was reminded suddenly of the child's game of Steps, the wonderful prickly feeling of tiptoeing across the room, ready to freeze into stillness the instant the leader whipped around. What would happen if he were to creep silently out of the tent? Would all the tiny noisemakers out there freeze in their tracks? Play statues? He chuckled at the idea, and then drifted off into sleep while he was still grinning at the joke.

There were no more dreams that night, and Mike woke with the sun on his face and a good feeling inside that he couldn't pin down. He lay in a warm, lazy half-doze, looking at the long shadows of the frozen spikes of grass that rimmed the tent door where he'd brushed the snow away.

Beyond the tiny picket-fence of stiff grass was the dead fire, white ash laced over the charcoal of not-quite-burned wood. He stretched his feet luxuriously down to the bottom of his sleeping bag and wriggled his toes. God, it was good to be alive!

That was it! That was the feeling he had woken with, a feeling as unfamiliar as an unexpected gift....

He dressed slowly, enjoying the crisp feeling of his jeans, the warmth and softness of his wool shirt, the clean dry socks. He scrambled down the river bank to splash his face and hands in the still-unfrozen water. The icy agony made him gasp, but it set his blood tingling, and by the time he had dried he felt even better.

He looked around as he dried off and combed his hair. No rush. No appointments, except with his deer, and that would come in its own good time. It was going to be a perfect day. The sky was a clear green deepening to blue directly overhead. The sun had a suspicion of a halo around it – no sun-dogs, just a warning that it was cold, but not dangerously cold.

He strolled back to his camp, which was beginning to have the familiarity of home. He was recognizing particular rocks, the suggestion of a track up from the river, a trailing wild rose that would catch your jeans if you didn't step just so.

He started the fire and looked for his coffee mug. In the tent, of course. He remembered the scurrying steps, the small crackles in the night, and looked around. Sure enough, the snow was covered with tiny prints. Squirrels, he wondered. Or some kind of mice or gophers that had not yet hibernated?

He made coffee and tipped instant oatmeal into the water remaining in the pan, set it at the edge of the fire and laid slices of bacon in the cast-iron frying pan. Later, as he spooned up mouthfuls of hot porridge and turned the bacon, he tried to work out some sort of strategy for the day.

Both mule deer and whitetail were at their most active close to dawn and dusk when they would be browsing on the tender shoots of aspen, willow, dogwood and mountain juniper, and whatever grass they might still find beneath the snow. During the rest of the day, especially during the

hunting season, for deer were no fools, they would be bedded down in some patch of brush from which only sheer
luck would flush them.

—

And he was only a beginner. He had decided that nothing
was going to tempt him to blaze away at a moving target and
chance wounding it rather than killing it outright. He was
going to be patient and wait until he had a clear stationary
target in his sights, no matter how tempting the alternative.

The best hide in this whole area was on the steep hill across
the river from the drinking place down by the gravel spit. There
he could wait out of sight and then just take his pick when they
came down to drink. If the river were only frozen across it
would be perfect. But it wasn't.

Regretfully he gave up the idea. If he got wet crossing to
a hide on the steep northern bank he'd freeze to death. No,
he would have to work the trails, the deer runs. Some of the
ones he had seen yesterday led uphill towards the fire road
that crested the ridge southwest of his camp. The deer
would find good browse up there, young saskatoons, aspen
and dogwood, sprouting vigorously away from the compe-
tition of the overshadowing spruce and pine of the deep
woods. His best bet would be to work his way uphill from
his camp, due west towards the fire road, so that his path
crossed the deer runs going up from the drinking place by
the gravel spit. When he found a likely-looking trail he'd
still-hunt along it until it brought him out on the cut, and if

in all that time he saw nothing, he would backtrack down the next trail.

He finished a large and leisurely breakfast. A whisky-jack hopped agitatedly from branch to branch at the edge of the clearing. He threw it a crust and it jumped down and snatched at the food, staring at Mike with its bold black eyes, its grey plumage ruffled in the breeze. There was an angry scream and a second arrived. Then a third. He tossed more pieces of bread. They were as greedy and brash as seagulls. When they saw there was no more they retreated to the trees at the edge of the clearing. He could feel their eyes on him, watching for an opportunity to steal.

He stretched and glanced at his watch. 10:28. He'd really overslept. A good hunter wouldn't miss the morning the way he had. Sunset would be at 4:59. That meant that hunting big game was no longer legal after 5:29. Anyway it would be dumb to be far from camp once the sun had set. In these hills it would get dark very fast, and he mustn't risk getting lost.

Right now the sun was well above the trees and almost uncomfortably warm on his head and shoulders. The deer would be seeking the shade and a place to ruminate. Between now and three or so there was little chance of seeing any game unless he happened to walk right on top of a deer. He decided to spend the rest of the morning getting his gear in perfect order. Then he'd have a light lunch and start tramping uphill towards the deer runs.

He took his gun from the tent and cleaned it lovingly. He'd only used it on targets at the rifle range, but he'd done all right there, he had an eye for it. And the rifle was a beauty. Brand new, it had cost a shocking eight hundred dollars. He'd have been happy with a second-hand one at a quarter of the price; but that was Dad all over. Only the very best for his son. It bothered Mike sometimes.

Now, by himself in the bush, he began to see some things more clearly. He could understand the feelings that made Dad spend too much money on things like this gun. It was the only way he could say what he felt. Why was it so hard for him?

He sat with the gun on his knee and the cleaning rag in his hand, and his thoughts drifted to home. He couldn't help feeling a bit guilty, thinking about them worrying. He'd been gone over twenty-four hours. Would they be making a fuss, calling the police? Or would they understand the note he'd left under his pillow: that he needed to be alone. To work things out. To get his trophy, though he hadn't told them that.

When I get home it'll be different, he promised himself. When I get home with my deer – a trophy head, please God let me bag a trophy – then they'll have to accept that I'm not a child any more, that they won't have to go on hiding things from me.

Why had they lied to him all year, he wondered. Oh, it was their way of protecting him, he could see that. But how could they have done it so easily, so readily? As if it were second nature. They'd never lied to him before that he could remember....

Out of the blue came a sudden flash ... grade one, himself

running into the house one Saturday afternoon, yes, it must have been a Saturday, so choked up with tears he could hardly talk.

"Joey says there isn't such a person as Santa, that I'm a baby to believe in him. Dad, he's a liar, isn't he? Isn't he?" He could remember getting hold of Dad's leg and shaking him, demanding the truth.

And Dad had told him that indeed there was a Santa, and that Joey was mistaken, you mustn't use words like liar, Mikey. Mother had backed him up. She'd washed his blubbery face and they'd all gone off to a movie matinee and seen an old Tarzan ... Tarzan and the ... he couldn't remember which one. But he could remember them sitting by the fire in the family room afterwards, eating Kentucky Fried Chicken right out of the bucket with their fingers.

And then going to bed surrounded with love and caring.... But he could remember now how betrayed he'd felt the very next December when he'd been snooping and had come across the brightly wrapped parcels in the parents' closet, and worst of all, the ultimate betrayal, the red and white Santa costume, as limp as a corpse, hanging in its plastic drycleaner's bag at the very back. Joey wasn't a liar at all, *they* were.

Funny how memory came sneaking back, sitting here in the quiet of the bush. There was the question of the Facts of Life. Mother had told him some story, and he'd felt pretty stupid when the grade two boys had compared versions. Or was it grade three? He could remember going home and telling the parents his new, somewhat garbled version of the truth, and they'd denied it flat. He could remember feeling relieved. Their version was so much tidier than the truth.

Looking back, it was really pretty funny. But why had they done it? Just a couple of silly incidents in a safe and happy childhood. Why should they bother him now? Maybe they weren't important. But looking back now, they were like signposts leading towards the dark wood of this last year.

They loved him. They wanted to protect him, but he couldn't let them do that any more. When he got back he was going to have to be strong enough to find a way past his own fear to his parents' fear for him, and somehow cancel that out. Could he do it? Could they find a new way of being close and truthful? He could sure as hell try, though it wasn't going to be easy.

Mike sighed. He got out the box of cartridges and loaded the rifle. He put a half-dozen extra in his breast pocket and checked his survival kit. It was a small tin box that fitted snugly into the lower pocket of his mackinaw. In it were half a dozen waterproof matches, flint and steel, snare wire, fishing lures and line. There were painkillers and antibiotic tablets, a razor blade, antiseptic, a sterile pad, adhesive tape and a few band-aids. Tea bags, bouillon cubes. Tiny packets of sugar, the kind you get on airplanes.

Theoretically one could survive indefinitely in the bush with the contents of this kit. It was like a lifejacket. But there was a feeling of false drama about the little box that made Mike feel foolish. He hesitated and then stuffed it into his left pocket. After all it wasn't heavy.

He checked his clothes. Climbing in the middle of the afternoon was going to be warm work, but as soon as the sun slipped into the shadow of the western hills the temperature would drop like a stone, and he'd have to be ready for it. He'd already got on a thermal undershirt and long johns tucked into his socks at the ankle. Jeans, a light wool shirt and a mackinaw with all its useful pockets would probably be more than warm enough for most of the day. His downfill was going to be a nuisance, but he'd have to take it for later. Then there was the Blaze Orange jacket and cap. That was a safety precaution more important than the survival kit. And it was the law.

He hadn't seen or heard a sign of another hunter since he'd turned onto the fire road, but that didn't mean that they weren't around. A good hunter wouldn't be seen or heard, stalking or still-hunting. But though the deer were unaware of the colour, to another hunter the fluorescent orange of the cap and jacket would be as visible as a stop sign. It was a nuisance wearing that extra layer, but it was better than lying in the bush with a bullet in your head.

With the jacket half on he hesitated. Maybe that would be a better way to go. It would be quick. The idea of lying under the trees on a soft bed of pine needles, slowly disintegrating, becoming one with the quiet forest, had a certain morbid attraction.

"You're crazy, Mike Rankin," he said aloud, startled by his own thoughts. "Sick!" He put the jacket on and did up the buttons. Then he checked everything again, as if he was telling himself, or God, if God was paying attention, that he didn't mean it, that he wasn't going to do anything stupid. There was the compass tucked into his breast pocket, the cord safely around his neck. Cartridges in the other breast pocket, survival kit over his left hip. Knife at his belt. His Wildlife and Big Game licence was tucked into the pocket of his shirt, safe but out of the way, together with the hunting tag. Had he forgotten anything?

He wasn't hungry, and he was itching to be off. In the end he didn't stop for lunch, but stuffed a couple of granola bars into his right pocket, kicked out the fire, picked up his rifle and his downfill and left camp. The jays watched him from their trees, staring like vultures. He saw them jump down to the ground as soon as he turned away. Well, they were going to be disappointed. He'd left no food scraps and nothing they could get into.

He struck uphill, almost due west. The slope wasn't too steep, but the bush was dense. He moved as quietly as he could through the deadfall wedged in between spruce, pine and low brush, conscious of the noise he was making, afraid that every whitetail in this part of Swan Hills was going to take off before he could get near them. It seemed an age before he came to a deer run.

There were clear hoofprints in the skiff of snow. Whitetail or muley? He wasn't sure. The deer run meandered from side to side around an area of deadfall, close to a thicket where long grass still poked dry above the snow. The prints all led upward, and slowly, as silently as he could, Mike followed them.

When he stopped there was no noise but the faint shiver of dead aspen leaves far overhead, though down here among the tree trunks he could feel no breeze. Which way would the wind carry his scent? If it was coming from behind him it would give a clear warning to all the resting deer ahead. They would drift quietly away and no matter how carefully he walked, they would always be gone before he got there.

He stared up at the sky until he was giddy. There just wasn't enough wind to tell the direction. The few golden leaves that still clung to the grey branches moved and rattled like a weathervane in a near calm, just twisting first to one side and then back to the other. Forget it.

He walked carefully on and then stopped to look around again. He remembered what Doug's dad had said. "You've got to walk with the same rhythm a deer does. Just meander along for a bit. Then stop. Stay perfectly still while you look ahead to your left and right. Then look again, closer this time. Keep your eyes peeled for something a little different, something out of place."

"Like antlers poking up," Mike had put in eagerly, and Mr. O'Reilly had laughed.

"You should be so lucky! More likely what you'll see is a patch of pale grey where the tree trunks are all dark, and where there's no light to account for that paler patch. Maybe you'll get lucky and see an ear flick. So you look a little harder. Use your scope. Move slowly. Wait. You still don't know if you've spotted a buck or just a doe. Okay. Let's say you've seen its antlers. You're sure it's a buck. Is it a whitetail or muley? You'd better not start to blaze away at something you don't have a licence for."

A patch of grey where no grey should be. The twitch of an ear. The horizontal line of back or belly in this shadowy shifting world of verticals....

Mike stopped. Gazed. Peered. Walked slowly on. The ground surface was very good. The snow made a thin carpet, just enough to cover the fallen aspen leaves so that they didn't crunch underfoot. The pine needles made a carpet that was always soft and silent. He put each foot down slowly, feeling for the ground from heel to toe before he took the weight off his other leg. His whole being concentrated on quiet. His heart banged against his chest wall. He tried to keep his breathing soft and relaxed. Even though he was moving slowly there was sweat on his forehead. He could feel a faint air chill against his damp face. Good. The breeze was on his side, carrying his scent downhill behind him.

His shoulder brushed against the outstretched fronds of a spruce branch, and the whisper of its needles against the nylon of his Blaze Orange jacket seemed so loud that he jumped and his fingers tightened on his rifle. Steady! Time for another look around.

There were deer runs everywhere, crisscrossing each other, all moving more or less up and down, between the river behind him and the fire road up ahead. Which trail would be the right one? He could be still-hunting up an empty trail. Or the deer could be hiding in every thicket, behind every tree, just laughing at him.

He began to feel jumpy. He found that he wasn't just looking ahead when he stopped, but over his shoulder as well. Down below him – he'd climbed farther than he realized, unaware of the gradient since he'd been moving so slowly – the valley was filled with shadows. In front of him it was definitely lighter. It wasn't his imagination. Yes, the dense spruce and pine were thinning out. There were more of the slim pale trunks of young aspen. He must be getting close to the fire road. Out there would be the best place to browse. The deer could munch at the occasional clump of grass or tender young sapling down in the forest, but to get enough food they'd have to get out where the browse was more plentiful, at the edges of the cut lines.

Mike stared at the ambiguous outlines of tree trunks and branches and shadows. There was nothing. He must have misjudged the area entirely, in spite of the fresh hoofprints and droppings. He moved forward again. At least he'd get out of the bush onto the cut and have a look around, plan where he'd be when the deer came up at twilight.

Without warning the area directly in front of him exploded into life. He saw flashes of grey and white, stick-thin legs, a glimpse of ears and antlers, the unbelievable momentary stare of an eye. Then there were deer leaping away from him in every direction.

He ran forward, crashing over dead branches and through tangles of brush, raising his gun, fumbling inexpertly with the bolt. Suddenly he was out on the cut, staring across the smooth snow-covered width to where the trees made a dark line at the far side.

The wind sighed coldly down the open cut, stirring dry weeds and grasses that poked stiffly up out of the snow. There was nothing in sight. Mike lowered his rifle and stared blankly around. His heart was pounding and his breath was coming hard, making little clouds of vapour in the cold air. Had he dreamed it? Had they really been there at all?

He felt a total fool. It had seemed so easy in all the books he'd read, even the way Doug had described it. He'd done everything right, up to that last minute. And then it had all come apart. There'd been deer all around him at a point-blank range and he hadn't even aimed his rifle!

Where the hell were they now? He jog-trotted through the rough grass of the cut until he was out in the middle. There was nothing to see but the marks of his own boots. He walked slowly back to the place on the deer run where it had all happened. There was their hiding place only a stone's throw from where he'd been standing, slap in the middle of a thicket of deadfall. He could see the heart-shaped cloven hoofprints cutting into the light snow. They'd gone in two directions after they'd exploded out of the thicket, to the right and left of him, not out into the cut where they'd be exposed to the rifle of any waiting hunter. They were smart all right. By the time he'd got his wits about him they'd melted right back into the bush.

Once his anger at his own stupidity had died down,

Mike began to feel cheerful. After all, he'd been on the right deer run. He'd surprised the deer as much as they had surprised him. They'd probably not gone far. They'd be hungry soon and ready for their evening meal. If he could just stalk one of them he might still get lucky....

He picked the deepest footprints, the heaviest deer, the one likely to have the best head, and set off doggedly, his footsteps quiet on the light snow cover. He remembered to walk as he had been told, slowly, with frequent pauses and no unnatural man-like rhythm to disconcert the sharp ears of his quarry.

The prints led north, parallel to the ridge of the hill and a little to the east of it. At first they were far apart, and the droppings were scattered, as though his deer – he had already begun to think of it as "his" – was moving fast. But he walked on, stopping to look around, pretending to move and think as an animal would, with no particular goal in mind, and after a while he noticed a clump of droppings all together, and then a place where grass had been freshly torn away.

His eyes were continually busy, on the trail, or casting to the left and right ahead, peering through the shadows for that different something that might be the outline of his deer. He never looked up. If he had, he would have noticed the storm clouds gathering, dark, with a yellow tinge – clouds that were heavy with snow. He peered at the ground, puzzled that it was becoming harder and harder to see. He stopped to look at his watch. Only four o'clock? Had his watch stopped? Why was it so dark? By the time he did think to look up, the snow was falling fast, drifting down between the trees, piling up along the branches. Covering up the trail of his deer. Covering up his own back trail.

FIVE

It happened between one moment and the next, between looking up to see the suddenly dark sky and the snowflakes caught up in the wind; and then looking back to where he had come from to see nothing at all. There was no trail, no north or south, no direction anywhere.

Mike felt as if he were trapped inside one of those little globe snow scenes that you turn upside down and shake to make the snow drift down. He turned and began to run, vaguely downhill, but within a dozen steps he caught his foot on a root and fell.

As he sprawled forward the precious rifle was jolted from his hand and fell forward into the snow. He scrambled to his knees, fighting to get his breath back, and his mind began to work again. He had actually panicked. Stupid! He could have broken his ankle doing a dumb thing like that. The rifle could have gone off. Anything could have happened. He took a shaky breath and tried to remember.... It was panic that was the killer in the bush. Not lack of food or water. Not the grizzlies. Just man, destroying himself with his own fear.

He got to his feet and picked up his rifle. Had he jarred the scope? When he was safely back at camp he would have to check it out. Lord, it had got cold all of a sudden! He tugged on his downfill jacket, zipping it up to the neck and fastening the storm-fly, pulling the nylon hood down over his head.

He crouched down against the wide trunk of a spruce tree, his back to the driving wind and snow, and tried to think. He was shivering. In the few minutes since the storm had started, before he'd had the wit to get into his downfill, the wind had driven the heat from his body. And it was still daylight out there. Soon the sun, somewhere out there behind that white mass, would set, and then the real cold would begin.

The only thing to do was to hole up where he was and light a fire, wait out the storm and pray it wouldn't last too long. If it were only later in the year he could dig a cave in a snow bank and settle into it, as snug as a bear. But now the snow was no deeper than his wrist, and though it was drifting fast in the fierce wind, as if eager to help, it was too soft and new to build anything. It would be like trying to build a cave in a mound of feathers.

Along the bare man-made cut the wind howled savagely. When he stood up, away from the sheltering tree trunk, it snatched the breath out of his mouth and forced itself icily into his lungs, inflating them like balloons. He couldn't breathe out, and had to turn round with his back to the wind before he could gasp out the freezing air and let his lungs refill slowly. He could never survive up here. He would have to get down lower, out of the worst of the wind, before he could make a shelter and light a fire.

Bent low, trying to watch where he placed each foot, conscious of the danger of turning an ankle, he fought his way downhill into the forest, away from the torrent of wind that rushed like a cataract down the fire road. He couldn't go far. Already his knees were numb and he could feel his whole body shaking inside his warm downfill. All he could hope for was to stumble on some cranny where he might have a fighting chance of lighting a fire.

He fell against a fallen tree, already nearly buried in drifting snow, and almost lost his gun again. His shin had whacked against the log, but he felt no pain – his legs were too cold. He felt along the tree; it was a big one, and where it had been torn from the ground in some previous storm there was a small natural cave of dirt and torn tree roots, protected from the worst of the wind by the upturned circle of the tree bole.

He propped his rifle against a root, out of the way, and began to scrape the snow from the ground. There wasn't much of it close against the roots, and beneath it the ground was frozen and coated with dead leaves. He gathered them hastily into a heap on the bare ground. Then he had to leave the shelter and face the wind again, feeling along the length of the fallen tree for branches that he could pull off and break up with his hands. If only he had the axe! But then he could hardly have used it safely when he couldn't see his outstretched hands in front of him.

With both arms full he fought his way back to the earthy cave and began to build his fire. Above him like an open stove lid the tree base hung, a matted circle of dirt and stones held together by a knitted mass of roots. More snow had eddied into his clear patch while he'd been gone, but not much, and right at the back the air was almost calm.

Mike broke the driest branches into small pieces, pyramided them over his heap of dry leaves, and built another pyramid of larger sticks on top of the first. He had to take off his mitts to get at the emergency kit, which was in the pocket of his mackinaw under his downfill. By the time he'd got it out and zipped up his downfill again his hands were stiff and clumsy with cold.

The matches – if only there were more of them! – were the wooden kind that will strike anywhere hard and dry and rough. He looked around his dirt cave and in the end struck the first one against the thigh of his bluejeans.

It caught, and he nursed the tiny flame close between his hands and set it carefully to the base of the pyramid against the dry leaves. It flared, orange, the only living coloured thing in his white globe world, and he crouched over it, his hands protecting the pyramid of sticks from sudden gusts of snow-filled wind. He felt an instant's wonderful warmth against the icy palms of his hands before the cold air came down on the flame like an overweight blanket and smothered it.

It was the cold. That was the trouble. But the wood was

warmer now and drier. There were still five matches in the emergency kit. The next time the flames lasted much longer. A piece of resinous bark flared and smoked. He lay down and blew at it gently, trying to revive the sparks into flame. His hands were clumsy blocks of ice and his jaw ached with the effort of not letting his teeth chatter.

But there still wasn't enough heat at any one time to overcome the heavy layer of cold air pouring down the hill. He took three matches, lit each in turn and placed them at the back and at the sides of his fire. Going for broke. But it worked. This time he could actually feel the warm air rising and fanning his face. It pushed back the cold air. It consumed greedily every small branch he fed to it. He knelt by the fire and pulled a bigger branch towards him and broke it into foot-long lengths, and fed them into the fire. The flames mounted, caught the wind and were torn away in smoke.

Mike sat cross-legged by his fire, his back as close as he could get to the torn tree base, his bare hands over the blaze. He undid his downfill and his mackinaw so that the heat of the fire could get at his freezing body. He stayed as close as he could get until he could feel his skin smart with the heat, and only then did he do up his mackinaw and downfill and put on his mittens.

Outside his half cave the wind blew and the snow whirled downhill in pillars of white that made the wind visible. He leaned back against the wiry mass of rootlets and dirt, his arms folded across his body, hugging the new warmth to him. He no longer trembled with cold and fear.

In fact he felt unbelievably sleepy, wind-battered and dazed. But he mustn't sleep. If he slept the fire would go out, and the fire was his life. If he could just get a hot drink, something to keep him awake ...

He thought of the emergency kit. It was a small deep aluminum box with a lid. He took off a mitt and emptied the contents of the box and stowed them carefully in the pockets of his downfill. He packed the box with snow and set it close to the heart of the fire. The snow melted fast to a bare centimetre of water, and he topped it up with more snow and let that melt and then refilled it a third time until at last he had enough boiling water for a drink.

There were bouillon cubes in the kit and he peeled the foil off one of them and crumbled it into the hot water, stirred it with a twig. When he lifted the box off the fire by its lid he could smell the hot spicy beef smell; but though his mouth was watering he had to wait until the metal had cooled enough so that he wouldn't burn his lips.

The drink was marvellous, hot all the way down. He ate the granola bars between sips. He could feel the energy coming back into his body in warm waves. He put more wood on the fire. His pile was almost used up. Soon he would have to get up and face the blizzard in search of more dry wood. Soon ...

His head dropped and his body jerked. His eyes flew open. The fire burned so fast with the wind fanning it. He put the rest of the wood on and watched the sparks fly up and whirl away on the wind with the snow. Just one more minute to get really warm and then he'd go for more wood. His eyes shut.

Whump! Something heavy slid past his face. Then there was wetness everywhere. At his feet a wet hissing. Darkness. No fire. In front of his crossed legs was a mound of fast melting snow. Water ran against his jeans and he had pulled back his legs and scrambled to his knees before he even understood what had happened.

He pushed away the wet snow that mounded over the place where his fire had been. He scooped it up carefully at first, and then frantically, scrabbling through wet charcoal for a remnant of living fire. How could it have gone so quickly, snuffed out between one second and the next?

Whump! A load of snow, wet, heavy and icy cold, slapped the back of his neck and slithered from his shoulders to the ground. He looked up through the whiteness of snow and wind and saw, dimly above him, the branches of an enormous spruce. Then he remembered.

Sometimes the gulf between theory and reality is like the Grand Canyon. Mike had *known* that when you build a hot fire beneath trees you must take care that the load of snow on the branches above, especially of trees with wide sweeping branches like spruce, doesn't become warm and unstable and avalanche down on your fire. He had known all about this. But he hadn't really known it. Not until now.

Now his fire was a blackness of wet charcoal on which the snow softly fell. His dry starter of leaves was long gone. He had one match left. And it was getting dark and even colder.

His mind reached back, bewildered, across the canyon of "if only" to the few minutes before when the fire had been blazing and he had been so warm and comfortable that he had actually dozed off. So warm.

The November storm gave no quarter. It snatched at his newly acquired warmth and left him shivering. He had to act and act now. He stood up and found a dead branch protruding through the snow, and poked and shook the branches of the big spruce until they gave up their load of snow. He wouldn't be caught that way again.

He kicked away the wet remains of his fire, picked out the few big pieces of charcoal and tucked them into a hollow at the back of his tree cave. Then he felt his way along the trunk of the fallen tree, afraid to leave it. If he moved even a few metres away he might never find his way back. His visible world had shrunk to this small white globe that contained the fallen tree, the cave at its roots and the spreading spruce above.

He tore away dead branches that protruded up into the air. They should be dry. He made three trips with his arms full of wood, and then he knelt out of the icy wind and broke the wood into short lengths, making a neat pile at the back of his cave.

Then he took his hunting knife from its sheath at his waist and peeled the bark from short lengths of dry wood and stroked the knife along the bare wood, feathering up small fibres until he had half a dozen fuzzy "starters." The book had said that it would always work, but he'd never tried it before on damp ground in the middle of a howling blizzard.

He remade his fire with the feathered wood at its heart. Then he took his last match. There was still the flint and steel in the emergency kit, which should give him unlimited chances, but he didn't have much faith in them. After all, how could he ever start a fire with a spark if he'd failed to do it with the flame of a match?

With enormous care he struck his last match along the thigh of his blue jeans, sheltered it with both bare hands, set it to the finely shaved furry pieces of wood at the heart of the fire. It caught with no trouble at all, and he crouched over it, sheltering it from the wind with his body.

The flame was beautiful, clear and gold, almost smokeless. It lit up a tiny world of hope within the circle of Mike's protecting body. It curled around the small wood, separated, hissed where it met the dampness of his old fire. Come on, he urged it, his hands curved around, willing it. Grow. Live. Save me.

The gold flame lasted for perhaps fifteen seconds, not nearly long enough to catch the rest of the wood. He wouldn't believe it. He crouched with his head sideways, his cheek grazing the bare ground. Gently he blew at his dead fire. In and out. In and out. But there was nothing. Not even enough ash to blow away.

Mike put his icy hands back into his mitts. For a moment despair crawled in with the darkness, but he pushed it away. He took his knife and began to shave more of the driest wood he could find, feathering it with even finer cuts. Then he doggedly rebuilt his fire.

In the left pocket of his downfill was the flint and steel from the emergency kit. It consisted of a small block of wood, about five centimetres long, fifteen millimetres wide and three millimetres deep. Set lengthwise along half the length of one side was a strip of flint; and in a slot within the wooden handle, like a sword in a scabbard, was the steel, a piece of metal like a short thick razor blade notched along one length.

Experimentally he stroked the notched side of the steel along the flint. The spark was enormous, lighting up the darkness, but for too short a time even to measure. But it had been there.

The secret was to be able to direct it, and to make sure that it hit something really flammable. Only what? Dried moss? The feathers from an old bird's nest? The textbook answers crowded Mike's mind. But he couldn't go exploring. That was sure. Whatever he found must be within the safety of his small sphere of sight and feel. He remembered the sugar packets that were part of the survival kit. If he could fill them with something and use them as starters ... He dug them out and ripped them open carefully, tipping the sugar onto his tongue. It melted and ran sweet down his throat. At least it would give him an extra bit of energy.

Another memory came back to him from across the theory/ reality gulf. He scraped the surface fluff off his jeans with the flat of his knife until he was able to fill one of the little paper packets with a soft ball of lint. And the other? His mackinaw was of brushed cotton, he remembered, and he undid his downfill and scraped at the fluff that had collected in the bottom of the pockets. There was a surprising amount, more than enough to fill the second sugar packet.

Now he had two fire-starters: soft, open-ended cushions of paper bulging with lint. Again he stroked the steel down the flint. Aiming was the problem. The spark seemed to jump out at random, a sudden spot of light that burned his eye and was gone, leaving a more intense dark behind, with an after-image of green dancing in the midst of it.

He tried to be patient and slow, to push away the fear that was rising like sickness in his throat, making him quick and clumsy. Again he stroked the steel down the flint. This time it caught. There was a tiny drift of smoke rising from one of the lint cushions. He tucked it carefully into the base of his fire, lay with his cheek against the icy ground, and blew. The cushion burst into flame and caught one of the feathered sticks. Before it could go out he lit his second pillow starter from the flame and thrust it into the other side of the fire. He shielded the small living thing, coaxed it into growth, fed it gently, slowly.

At the trailing edge of the storm that was then passing over the Swan Hills the winds lessened. Instead of driving straight out of the west they became more influenced by the terrain over which they were passing. So it happened that at that moment the wind faltered for an instant, and when it resumed it blew along the natural channel dug between two hills by the Freeman River.

That was what actually happened. To Mike it seemed

that some deliberate and cruel fate sent the wind backing into the northwest with a sudden gust that caught the one spot where his fire, under the base of the tree, was not protected by the natural cave or by his body. There was a sudden gust, and the fire was out.

It was hard to believe that all his work could have been so quickly and easily undone. He shrank his cold body into the smallest possible space among the torn roots of the fallen tree. He began to feel colder than he had ever felt in his life. He was shivering uncontrollably and he felt rather sick. Hypothermia ... he'd read about *that*.

Before long he would have hallucinations, as the cold began to affect the operation of his brain. By then the chilling of his inner body would be irreversible, out here, alone, with no help, no fire. Soon he would drift into sleep. He might tear off all his clothes first, as his icy brain misinterpreted the signals of his body, and told him that he was hot, boiling hot, as if there were a heat wave. He'd read of people being found like that in the middle of a Canadian winter, frozen stiff and naked at the end of a trail of clothing. But naked or clothed, either way there would be sleep. And sleep would merge by degrees into unconsciousness, and unconsciousness into death.

I don't want to die! He hurled a silent shout up into the uncaring sky. He knew it was uncaring, that no one was listening, because he had been screaming the same silent phrase ever since last Christmas, and it hadn't helped.

He had had six weekends of pain and nausea during the initial treatment. He had thought that maybe you could get used to anything, but that wasn't true. He never got used to the IVs. And those nightmare weekends coloured everything else that happened to him. It was as if there were an invisible wall between himself and everyone else – parents, school friends, even Doug.

Classes weren't too much of a problem. He followed his timetable and moved from room to room. Most of his spares were taken up with the homework he'd missed on weekends. But the rest was ... loneliness.

At first the phone would ring as usual on Friday evenings. "Hey, we're all going down to the park to skate. The ice is good. Coming?"

He'd remind them that he had to be in bed early and off to the hospital in the morning.

There'd be a pause. "Gee, Mike, sorry. I forgot. See you Monday."

"You bet. Have a good time."

After a couple of weeks they stopped calling. On Mondays they'd talk about the weekend before going to class, and again he felt excluded. It wasn't their fault. It wasn't anyone's fault.

Doug used to drop by on evenings when there wasn't too much homework. They played rummy until they were bored.

Then Dad bought a game of Atari with all the extras. It took a lot more concentration than rummy.

"Hey, I beat you again."

"Sorry. Not thinking."

"You tired?"

"Nope." Mike shifted restlessly on the family room rug.

"We could stop if you'd rather do something else."

"Oh shut up being so bloody thoughtful!"

"You know, Mike, you're a real pain in the ass this evening."

"You don't have to stay."

"I sure don't."

Mike stopped glaring at the television screen and glared at the fire instead, "It's just ... it's getting on my nerves. Not just the treatment, you know, though God knows that's bad enough. But the tests, the blood samples. It's like having final exams every week of your life. You kind of hold your breath and wonder if you're doing okay. I hate it." His lips trembled. He stared at the fire.

"But you are getting better?"

"I guess so." Mike blew his nose hard. "They don't tell me a lot."

"Not even that Dr. Gage?"

"Uh-uh. You know, I really thought he was a good joe. Oh, maybe he is. Maybe it's all in my mind...."

"What is?"

"This feeling I've got that whenever I try to pin him down to what's really wrong with me, he has to rush off to see someone else."

Doug thought about it. "Maybe they don't know and

they're embarrassed to tell you. Hey, I read something in the paper the other night, about why they put initials on a patient's chart. Like GOK."

"What's that for?"

"God Only Knows. Maybe that's what's wrong with you."

"That's really comforting. Thanks."

"Any time. Want to play cribbage?"

"I dunno. Might as well, I suppose."

⎯

Then two weeks before Christmas Dr. Gage gave him the news. "No more weekends in hospital. Your count is really good, Mike. Everything looks great."

At first he just stared. He couldn't believe it. Then he began to grin, and then laugh. Then he was out in the lobby where Mother was waiting for him, and she saw his face and ran clean across the lobby and hugged him. And they were both almost crying. Which was idiotic.

"D'you think my hair'll grow back by Christmas?" He looked at himself in the visor mirror as Mother drove home.

"Two weeks? That's not much time. Maybe. We could buy you a wig if you liked, for parties and things."

"Sure, Mom. Me in a wig? Hoo! Oh, I guess it doesn't matter anyway. People are used to the way I look. I don't care any more. It's finally over, no hospitals ever again. Gee, I feel so great I could shout!" He rolled down the car window and leaned out. "Hey, world, I feel great!"

Mother and Dad went hog wild over Christmas preparations, even worse than usual. They filled the house with mistletoe and swags of evergreen and red velvet ribbon, and decorated the huge tree that stood in the big bay window of the living room. And parcels piled up underneath. Mike had to make up his mind what to get for Mother and Dad. Doug. All his other friends. He'd hardly touched his allowance since November, so money was no barrier. Except for Gloria. She was still going out with that grade twelve guy – he didn't know his name, didn't want to. It would have been so terrific to get something spectacular for Gloria and just see her face....

The days zipped by, what with exams and being free to go out on weekends again. At first he didn't notice that anything was wrong. Until the day he came into the living room and found Mother in tears. A glass bauble had fallen from the tree and smashed, and she was trying to pick up the pieces, only she was crying and couldn't see what she was doing.

"Hey, Mom, did you cut yourself?" He took the pieces carefully from her and looked at her hand. "No, it's okay. Hey, it's only an ornament. I'll get you another, bigger and better."

"This was the one my sister gave me the Christmas after you were born."

"I'm sorry, Mom. Look, I'll get you another one to celebrate my being well again, and years from now it'll be just as special, and you'll be showing it to your grandchildren."

He kissed her cheek, expecting her to laugh and tell him how silly she'd been. Instead she clung to him for a moment, then kissed him back and went out of the room, leaving him alone, puzzled, to pick up the slivers of glass and wrap them in a kleenex.

He became aware of an atmosphere of edginess. It wasn't his imagination. Several times he came on them sitting silently in the living room or the kitchen. When they saw him they'd be all smiles again.

"Hi, fella, you look great this morning."

"All set for your math exam, darling?"

Chatter like that. But he had the strange feeling that as soon as he left, the smiles would fade and the silence would come back.

Were they splitting up? The crazy thought brought him up short. Yet was it so crazy? Half the guys in his grade were living with only one parent, or with a new stepfather or mother. But not Mother and Dad.... He began to watch them more closely. He even read the labels on the gifts beneath the tree.

"To Anita, with all my love, George." And "To my dearest husband, with love from Anita." It *sounded* all right, didn't it?

In the end he couldn't stand the tension any more. He laid it out before them over Sunday brunch, lazy and late with Mother making waffles.

"Are you two planning to get divorced?" It came out more crudely than he'd expected, but it got their attention all right, and their astonished expressions told him that he was nuts, even before their protestations.

"But what on earth gave you the *idea*, Mike?" Mother asked.

Mike fidgeted with the syrup container until she reached out and took it from him. "I don't know," he muttered. "I just had this feeling that you were hiding something from me, and I couldn't think what else it could be."

He looked up in time to see a look of guilt flash between them, so quick that he wondered if he'd imagined it. "You *are*. I knew it."

"Come on, Mike, you're getting paranoid in your old age," Dad said, and threw down his napkin. "Lord, why am I sitting here? I'm supposed to be meeting a client in a couple of hours. Good prospect out in the west end."

Mother gave him a look that Mike didn't understand. Then she jumped to her feet too and began to clear the breakfast table.

"What are you doing today, Mike?"

"I should study. English exam on Tuesday. The last of the lot."

"I won't disturb you then, dear. I'll leave a lunch in the fridge and you eat whenever you feel like it."

He went to his room feeling dismissed, his questions unanswered. It was on his mind all Monday. Tuesday too. He didn't do that well on the exam, he was sure. Thinking about the parents kept getting in the way of *Julius Caesar*. They were lying. He knew it. But what about?

On Wednesday morning he had to go for a check-up at the hospital. In and out, just a once-over and a blood sample. But nothing much was happening at school now that exams were over....

"Can I talk to you, Jim?"

"Sure." Dr. Gage came back and sat on the edge of the examining table, as if there was no hurry in the world.

"Something's wrong," Mike said slowly.

"With you? Something you haven't told me about?" He was suddenly alert, like a dog after a scent.

"No, not me. The parents." He was silent. It was hard to put into words without sounding paranoid, the way Dad had suggested. "I keep feeling they're hiding something."

"Any idea what?" The question was casual.

"I thought maybe they were breaking up. But it isn't that. I asked and I'm sure ..."

"So?"

"So I've been thinking ... I wondered ... well, you've always been pretty straight with me, Jim. I thought maybe you could help."

"I'm here to help you. You know that. But ..."

"Am I cured?"

Jim Gage put his hands in the pockets of his white coat, shifted and stretched. His smooth babyish face never gave anything away, Mike realized. He suddenly wondered what the other patients thought of the doctor. He'd never seen any, isolated as he had been in the splendour of his private room.

"Am I?" he repeated, and felt his heart thump hard.

"Cure is a word doctors hate to use, Mike. Except for things like appendices that don't grow back once they've been removed! You're extremely well and I'm very pleased with you. Isn't that enough? It's been a tough six weeks for you, but it's over. Finished with school? You'll be looking forward to the holidays, I bet."

"But ..." Mike stared at Jim Gage. The doctor looked steadily back, his face smooth.

"Look, Mike. Your parents have been worried to death about you. You realize that, of course. Perhaps what you're picking up is the emotional backlash from that. Say, I'm sorry, Mike, but I must go. I'm late for rounds. Happy Christmas."

He held out his hand and Mike shook it automatically. Then the doctor left and he wandered aimlessly out. It was grey and threatening snow. A heavy cold sort of day. He shivered inside his downfill.

It's not my imagination, he thought. There is something they're all hiding from me. Something really horrible like leprosy or ... he couldn't think of anything worse. Or perhaps Doug was right. Maybe it was GOK. God Only Knows.

He turned back to the door to Outpatients and then hesitated. Dr. Gage had left, and he knew by now that he could never get anyone else to talk. He stood on the side-walk while people hurried by, pushing past him. Then, without giving himself time for second thoughts, he caught the next downtown bus and got off at the library.

It had something to do with his blood, he knew, so he started at the Subject catalogue and went on from there. There were shelves and shelves of books about diseases of the blood. He hadn't realized before just how many things could go wrong. Really, it was a miracle that most people were healthy.

He leafed through book after book, bogged down by words he had never heard before, but going doggedly on. The trouble was that the symptoms he had seemed to be common to so many diseases – he was no longer surprised at the battery of tests he had first had in the hospital. It was too bad that they hadn't told him what was going on. Knowing about it would have made it all much more interesting and bearable. But all the time they'd treated him as if he were just a kid.

He had a pile of books as high as his arm, and a headache. He was about ready to call quits when a familiar word jumped off the page at him. Vincristine. That was the stuff Dr. Gage had started him on, the poisonous junk that had made him so sick. He'd never forget that name. But what was it for? He went to the librarian and was introduced to *The Compendium of Pharmaceuticals and Specialties*, an enormous dictionary of every drug known to man. And it was in this book that he found the truth that everyone from the parents to the doctors and nurses had been hiding from him for the past two months. Vincristine was used specifically in the treatment of acute lymphocytic leukemia.

It was lucky that he'd been sitting down at one of the reading desks when he came across this. He had the peculiar feeling that the blood was draining down his body and into his feet and out, as if someone had pulled a plug. He knew all about leukemia. That was what Ali McGraw had in *Love Story*. It was a one-way street.

Gradually the blood started to go back to where it

belonged, and after a while he was able to get up. But he felt numb all over. He went out of the library and drifted across the square towards the shopping centre. The wind was icy and only a few people were skating to the cheerful music in the square.

He wasn't really hungry, but he felt cold and hollow inside, and when he passed a restaurant with warmth and lights, he went in and found a nook at the back. It was comfortable and quietly expensive. When the waiter came he ordered a reuben sandwich. He'd have asked for a beer, but though his illness had made him look older, he wasn't sure if he looked eighteen and it would be embarrassing in a place like this to be asked for I.D.

The sandwich arrived, thick and gooey, stuffed with shaved corned beef and sauerkraut, dripping with melted cheese. He found himself bolting it down, hardly chewing. The taste wasn't important. Only to try and fill the hollowness inside him. When he had finished he was sorry he had eaten so fast, since the waiter came back with unnecessary promptness. But it was lunch hour and there was a line-up waiting beyond the cash register.

Mike didn't want to leave. There was a comforting cave-like feeling about the place. The candies on the tables were set in rose-coloured glasses, and the banquettes and deep chairs were upholstered in dark warm red. Outside he could glimpse the real world past the curtains. Black and white and cold.

He ordered a cup of coffee and sipped it slowly. When it was finished he asked for a refill and spun that out as long as he dared. Then the waiter came, pad in hand, and Mike regretfully rose to leave.

Outside it was beginning to snow again. He didn't want to go home. Mrs. Holden would be busy in the kitchen preparing for tonight's party. Mother would probably be at the hairdresser and Dad would be out putting together some elaborate land deal.

In the end he went back to the library. He dreaded finding out any more about this thing he'd got, and yet he couldn't leave it alone, the way you can't keep your tongue from probing a sore tooth.

It didn't take him very long to find out that there was more than one kind of leukemia – that some were pretty bad, but others a good deal better. Maybe he didn't have to be like Ali McGraw. Maybe he wasn't going to die!

He had to know. Without thinking about the fact that it was late afternoon, he ran out of the library and caught a bus that would take him by the hospital. The girl at Outpatients stared. "But you were in this morning, weren't you?"

"Yes. But I've got to see Jim – Dr. Gage – again. It's really important."

"He's left for the holidays. Would you like to see ..."

"No. I'll try and get him at home."

"You'd better phone first ...," she called after him. But he didn't listen.

It was disconcerting to find Jim Gage wearing the same kind of silly paper hat that he hated at his parents' parties. But then he saw, in the living room beyond, a cluster of small girls in organdy frocks and solemn boys in neat jersey suits, and he realized that he'd butted in on a family children's party.

He stammered an apology and dithered on the doorstep, not wanting to intrude but not wanting to go away either. An eddy of wind sent snow flurrying into the house. The doctor pulled him in, showed him where to leave his boots, and took his downfill from him.

"Back here. My study. Sit down and get warm. I'll be back in a jiffy. I'll just tell Madeline and make sure she can cope."

The study was small with deep leather chairs and lots of books. There were logs in the fireplace but they weren't lit. Mike walked up and down looking at the titles of the books, not taking them in.

When Jim Gage came back he had discarded the paper hat. He went over to the fireplace and put a match to the logs. They were the artificial kind made of chemically treated paper and they burned at once with green and blue flames.

"Come on. Sit." He pointed to one of the chairs before the fire, and took the other. "What's happened?"

Mike started a rambling apology about coming over uninvited.

"Forget that. Go on. Spit it out."

"I know what's wrong with me." Mike stared straight into the hazel eyes. They didn't change or turn away. They regarded him calmly.

"And what's your conclusion, Mike?"

"Acute lymphocytic leukemia. That's right, isn't it?"

"That's it. Did your parents finally tell you? I felt they

should have, all along."

"The parents? You've got to be joking. No, I found out for myself. Went to the library and dug around. I remembered the name of that first drug ..."

"Vincristine?"

"Yeah. That was the clue. I wonder why you let that slip."

"I don't know, Mike. Perhaps subconsciously I hoped you'd do what you did."

"Why didn't you just tell me the truth? Didn't I deserve that much?"

Jim Gage nodded. He took out his pipe. Spoke slowly while he rasped it clean, blew through it, filled it, tamped the tobacco with a gentle thumb. Lit it, and spoke between puffs.

"Yes, you did. And I apologize. Believe me, Mike, it was none of my doing. If only ... if only your parents would have given me permission ... to discuss your case honestly with you."

"But it's my life, what there is of it."

"It certainly is. And I respect you and your right to know. But even though you are a very adult sixteen, technically you are still a minor. They had the right to refuse to allow me to discuss your case with you. I really did try to persuade them, you know."

Mike nodded. "And you came right up against a stone wall, right? No, more like a foam rubber wall. But ... well, now I know, don't I ... so will you tell me the truth now?"

"Of course. I'll have to tell your parents I've talked with you – I hope you don't mind?"

"Sure. Maybe it'll help. I mean, if they know I know. Look,

Jim, I did a lot of reading down at the library. It was hard to understand, but I got the idea that my chances depend on which kind of cells are affected ... that that's what a lot of those blood tests were all about. Is that right?"

"Substantially, yes."

"Well then, I want to know where I stand. What my chances are."

"Are you sure? Don't you think you've got more than enough to handle right now without a mess of details? Oh, I can hear what you're saying: 'Lay it on me. I'm ready.' But maybe tomorrow or the next day, when some of the initial shock has worn off, you'll wish I hadn't."

"It's *that* bad, eh?"

"There you go. I don't know what 'that bad' is in your mind. I know what type of ALL you have. I can look up the statistical prognosis. But that won't help. You're not a statistic, Mike. You're a person. If you want me to tell you for sure if you'll be alive a year from now, or five years from now, well, I can't do it, because I just don't know."

"I see." Mike tried to smile.

"I don't think you do. You could be in complete remission right now, or in one that might last for years. On the other hand you could be in trouble next week, next month. But that's not a death sentence either, Mike. New drugs are coming out all the time, we're learning more and more every day. And I'm not trying to be evasive."

"Okay. Okay. I believe you." Mike suddenly felt shivery in spite of the fire. "I guess I came here without stopping to work out what I felt. Maybe I was hoping you'd tell me I'd made a mistake. That it wasn't leukemia at all. Or that it was some kind I'd be sure to get better from."

"I'm sorry, Mike. I wish the truth were that easy to take. Can you understand now a bit how your parents must be feeling? How they've only been trying to protect you?"

Or themselves, Mike thought, and then thought again: It's not their fault if they can't take the truth. He found that he was fighting tears. He stared into the bright flames and clenched his fists until the nails bit painfully into the palms of his hands.

"I don't want to die!" The words suddenly burst out of him and he began to cry, hoarsely, painfully.

"I suppose none of us wants to." Jim Gage spoke quietly, once Mike's sobs had quietened. "But we're all going to. Our cells start to deteriorate before we're even out of infancy. From then on it's only a matter of time."

"Time! I haven't had any time at all. I haven't started living. It's not fair...."

"Life isn't fair, Mike. Or unfair. It just is. It's a gift whether it's long or short. Perhaps it's the way we live, the quality of our life, that counts, rather than the quantity."

"I'll bet you've made that speech a hundred times before," Mike jabbed spitefully. "You must get used to it."

There was a silence before Jim Gage answered. Then he spoke slowly, almost reluctantly. "No, actually I haven't. You're the first teenage patient I've had. Mine are usually much younger. Pre-schoolers, or kids in the primary grades."

"Little *kids?*"

"Yes. That's when ALL usually starts. You're a latecomer."

"How do they take it?"

"Amazingly well. I'm always surprised at how trusting and brave these young kids are. Talking to them is a very humbling experience."

Mike felt ashamed and tired and confused all at once, He stood up. "I won't keep you. You've got this party thing."

"Don't worry about that. Are you all right? Shall I drive you home? Talk to your parents?"

"No. Not now. I'm fine. I just ... need to think. I'll talk to the parents later ... when I've got myself together."

He escaped from Dr. Gage's house, past the streamers and balloons and high voices singing "Oranges and Lemon."

I don't want to die. He felt like screaming it out loud to the leaden, snow-filled sky. To the people scurrying by on last-minute shopping before the stores shut for the holiday....

I don't want to die.

Six

I don't want to die! It was a cry within himself that jolted
Mike out of his frozen stupor. His brain began to work
again, to remember things he had learned and then forgotten. He staggered to his feet, peering up through the driving
snow and the gathering dark at the great spruce that grew
on the slope directly above him, its spreading branches
overshadowing the tree-root cave. It was already covered
with snow again, like a white pyramid. On hands and knees
he crawled up the slope under the fan-like sweep of its
lower branches.

Underneath, close to the great trunk, he was in a different
world, one that was dry and snowless and almost still. It was
also very dark, and he put his hand up to protect his eyes from
jabbing branches. Something brushed the back of his hand,
something like a heavy spider's web. He caught at it and got a
handful, and held it close to his face to see.

It was a lichen – dry, ugly stuff. He remembered its
name ... Old Man's Beard, that was it! He felt as triumphant

as if he'd just got a hundred on a quiz. It grew, he remembered, like coarse grey hair from the branches of old spruces, and as a fire-starter it was the best!

He gathered into a pile all he could reach, plucking it by feel. Then he broke off all the short branches and dead spurs he could find. They were as dry as midsummer, deep under the umbrella of the wide-spread branches.

He backed out, his arms full of his precious load, and slid down through the drifting snow to his tree-root cave. This time he was going to be very sure. Once he had arranged the new fire to his satisfaction he took one of the cartridges from the breast pocket of his mackinaw, slipped off his mitts, and began, very very carefully, to ease the bullet out.

It was a dangerous trick. You had to have just enough pressure. Not too much. If you squeezed too hard or rocked the tip of the bullet too violently you might set off the primer – and then goodbye hands and face. So Mike held his breath and wiggled the bullet free very carefully. If only his hands weren't so cold ...

There! The bullet was out, exposing the open cartridge filled with powder. He tapped it gently over his fire, and made a little trail from its centre towards him. He did it with care, like a finicky chef seasoning a dish. No haste this time. When the cartridge was empty he threw it and the primer away into the snow.

Again he took out the flint and steel. He pointed the flint towards the powder trail and drew the steel sharply along its edge. The spark seemed enormous, but the wind caught it and whipped it away. He moved his hands closer, trying to keep his face well back. He'd no idea exactly how it would behave if and when it caught.

Once more he drew the steel down fast, with a little curling flick at the end of the stroke. The spark landed squarely on the powder trail. There was a flare. Hot golden sparks flew in all directions. There was hot flame and smoke and a smell like fireworks. The grey lichen flared. With a roar the intense heat engulfed the pile of dry wood.

With shaking hands Mike slid the steel into its tiny scabbard and put the container safely into his pocket. Then he began once again to tend the fire. He piled on more fuel and then stood up and knocked all the snow flying sideways from every branch of the big spruce that could possibly be close enough to avalanche down onto his precious fire.

He set the small tin full of snow to melt and when it had melted he added more snow until he had a good cupful. There was a tea bag in the emergency kit. Tea was better than soup for keeping awake and alert. He should have realized that before.

The wind was definitely dying. The snow fell almost straight down now, big flakes with beautiful six-sided crystal spikes. That should mean that the temperature was rising a bit. He sipped the tea, as hot as he could get it down. His inside still felt as if there was a lump of ice in it, and hunger was making him feel a little sick. He fed the fire and drank the hot tea and planned the sumptuous menu he would cook when he got back to camp.

Human nature was certainly weird. He had escaped to the Swan Hills with a half-formed idea in his mind that if he didn't get his deer then maybe he wouldn't go back. He'd even played with the idea of death at the hands of some careless hunter. But when it came right down to the crunch, life won again.

Life would always win, he discovered. Not that death wasn't real, all right. And the way Dad and Mother tried to deny it didn't make it any the less real. But maybe it was that if you were strong enough to face up to death, then life became more real too. That must be the way the little kids coped – Dr. Gage's other patients. Only they didn't waste all this time and energy worrying about it and putting it into words. They just went ahead and lived it. Mike didn't know what life meant for the little kids, but for him it was the dream of getting that trophy head. And it had all begun with Doug....

Doug had seen him through. When Mike had got home from Dr. Gage's house on the Wednesday before Christmas he had decided that he'd come right out and tell the parents that he knew what was wrong with him. Leukemia. There. It didn't have to sound that bad, did it? Not a death sentence. Not necessarily. Jim Gage had explained about him being in remission, and how good it was, even though it didn't mean being cured. He had to live fully and hopefully. He could only do that if they helped him, if they all worked at it together ...

But his courage failed him as soon as he got inside the door.

"Oh, there you are, Mike. I was beginning to worry. Where have you been? Mrs. Holden's keeping your supper hot for you."

"Aren't you and Dad going to be home this evening?"

"It's the company Christmas party, remember?" His face must have shown his disappointment. "Dad has to go. But I'll stay home if you want."

Why hadn't he said yes? It would have been the chance for a quiet talk together. After they'd left and he'd finished his supper he prowled around all at loose ends. He could have kicked himself for putting off the moment another day. He'd blamed them for doing it, and now here he was, doing it too.

Doug phoned him next morning and impulsively Mike said, "Can you come out for coffee?"

"Sure."

"I'll meet you at Country Style in half an hour."

Over coffee and doughnuts Mike told Doug. It had been a good idea picking a public place to talk about it for the first time. After all, you can't break down and howl in a crowded coffee shop. Mike kept his eyes on the table while he talked. He could see Doug's hands, breaking his dough-nut into tiny pieces all over his plate.

"Hey," said Doug, when Mike stopped talking. "I'm glad you told me. It's shitty luck, happening to you. I'm really sorry."

Mike nodded. He managed a grin, though his face felt all stiff and peculiar. He cleared his throat, "I haven't told the parents."

"Huh? Oh yeah. You mean tell them you know."

"I was going to last night, but I got cold feet."

"This remission thing – is it ... is it the same as being cured?"

"Not really. They have to keep checking my blood. If I'm clear for five years or so, well, that's almost as good as being cured."

"We'll work on that idea."

"Yeah. But not playing games. Not pretending."

"No B.S. I promise. I guess that's the trouble with your parents."

Mike nodded and got up to refill his cup. "That's it."

"You'll just have to come right out and tell them you know."

"Yeah." He paused. "Christmas Eve today. I'll wait till after Christmas."

"You'll tell them then."

"Sure I will."

—

Christmas Day was on Friday. He didn't manage to talk to them until Sunday. A lazy brunch. Mrs. Holden was on holiday and Dad lit a fire in the family room fireplace while Mother made waffles. It was cosy, all of them together. Mike looked at Dad munching away. He should watch his diet, he thought fondly. He's getting a bit of a paunch. And Mother, looking awfully young in a velvety kind of robe, with her hair loose.

He swallowed a corner of waffle and took a swig of coffee. "You know," he began carefully, "if I'm still in this remission by August, wouldn't it be great to rent an RV and take a camping holiday together."

It took a while to penetrate. They just looked at him. Mother turned a little white. Dad put down his coffee mug on a lacquered table. "We could go across to Pacific Rim Park. Maybe down into Washington. It'd be fun," he went on.

"Yes, why don't we do that," Mother said slowly. "What do you think, George?"

Dad didn't answer her. "Has Dr. Gage been talking to you?"

"I've been talking to him. I found it out by myself, that I had leukemia, and I made him give me the details." There, it was out. Suddenly he felt much better. He took a swig of coffee. "Mom, I could really use a few more waffles."

"You'll burst." She smiled, but only with her lips. Her eyes looked scared. Well, it was bound to take them a while to get used to the idea of being honest with him. He'd have to give them time.

But really it was a relief to get back to school after New Year's. He felt as if he was picking up almost where he'd left off in October. He wasn't on the senior team any more, he'd just missed too much, but that was all right. There was the Gun Club. Movies and pizzas, skating and bowling. Time just shot by. And at last his hair was growing back. He went to the school dances but not with anyone special. He made up his mind that he wasn't going to get involved again. Not yet. Not till he felt really safe.

In February grade eleven planned a ski trip to Jasper.

"No way," said Dad, when Mike brought home the consent form.

"It's just for four days, Dad. I'll pay for myself."

"Don't be an idiot! As if I'd grudge the money."

"Then why not?"

"Your health. I don't want you ..."

"Dad, I feel great. Ask Dr. Gage if you don't believe me. D'you know my last platelet and white cell counts?"

"Of course I know them."

"Well, then."

But Dad just shook his head and wouldn't budge. He tried taking the form to Mother, but that didn't work. He phoned Dr. Gage, who phoned the parents. He begged. He sulked. In the end he had to stay at home while everyone else in his grade went off to Jasper.

"This can't keep happening," he argued. "I've got to live my own life."

But he couldn't get past "We know what's best for you."

Might as well be dead, he thought bitterly, and then took back the thought quickly: I didn't mean it, honest. In case anyone was listening.

—

In March Dr. Gage broke the news that his white cell count was way up and his platelets getting low. That the pills he'd taken had stopped being effective.

"But there are plenty more drugs in our arsenal, Mike,"

he told him bracingly. "We'll try them all, in turn, in combinations, until we find the ones that do the trick for you."

It was like being freed from prison, pardoned and then suddenly sentenced again. When the nurse at Admitting clipped the name tag on his wrist he could almost hear the gates clang shut. To make it worse he still felt great. Not like last time. It *had* to be a mistake.

He didn't feel great for long. The drugs they tried this time made him really sick and he had to stay in the hospital for days that seemed to last forever, taking nauseating drugs and trying to eat and not being able to.

Jim Gage seemed to be always there when he needed him. He told him what the drugs did and explained about his white cells. It was like a war, really, with good guys and bad guys, and different strategies for winning. Thinking about it like that helped somehow.

But in the end he and the darkness were alone together. It was his darkness and there was no one he could really share it with. If only he could talk properly to Mother and Dad. It ought to be all right now. Why couldn't they listen when he talked to them....

"Mom, I'm sorry."

"What about, Mikey?"

"I was so rude to you that day my hair fell out. I was rotten."

"Don't think about it, darling. It never happened." She kissed his forehead but he twitched away irritably. It *had* happened. How could he forget. There was so much to be said, just in case ...

"Dad, look, if I don't get through this time ..."

"Don't talk like that, Mike. You'll be fine. There's no doubt."

"But if. I just wanted to say ... I never told you ... I really want to do well, go to university. Maybe be a lawyer. Make you proud of me."

"You'll make it, son. University too. Stop worrying."

How could he ask them to help him fight the dark when they wouldn't admit that the dark was there?

Then one evening Doug turned up. Heaven knows how he'd wangled his way in. But there he was, red-faced, grinning from ear to ear, carrying the most monstrous parcel Mike had ever seen.

"How did you ... ? And what the hell is *that?*"

"It's for you. Maybe not here. Might give the nurses a fit. But something to look forward to, you know."

"But what is it?"

"Hang on a minute." Doug dumped the package on the foot of the bed, nearly crushing Mike's feet. He began to disentangle the yards of string that were wound around the parcel.

"Okay, wait for it." He loosened the paper. "Ta-tum!"

"Wow!" Mike stared at the mounted mule-deer head, a four-pointer with a spread of maybe fifty centimetres. "It's yours? Really? How? When?"

"That last weekend in November. When you couldn't come. I wanted to surprise you with it at Christmas, but it took this long to mount. D'you like it?"

"It's terrific."

"It's yours, man."

"Uh-uh. No way. You bagged it, not me. But thanks."

"You're sure?"

"Sure I'm sure. If I ever have a trophy on the wall it'll be mine."

Doug looked relieved. "It'll look pretty good in the rumpus room, don't you think? Mom won't let me have it in the living room, even though it's probably the biggest I'll ever get."

"It's *huge.* Is it a record?"

"Don't I wish! But for Swan Hills really good."

"That place we looked at on the map?"

"Yeah. Up close to the Freeman River. Hard to get at in the old station wagon. Dad's saving for a four-by-four. We'll have that for next year."

Next year. Mike closed his eyes on the pain. Then, "Go on." He managed a grin. "Tell me exactly how you got it."

"Well, we didn't see a thing on the Thursday, though there were signs everywhere. So on Friday Dad found a place, a little rise, well treed, but not as thick as the bush around it, just cross crossed with tracks. We hid there all day but we didn't see a blessed thing. Then just before sunset, just when the deer'd be moving again, this squirrel spotted us."

"Game over?"

"You bet. You never heard such a din. All we could do was trek back to camp half frozen."

"You must have been mad."

"No point. Dad says it's all part of the game. If you can't

learn patience you might as well forget it. Anyway, we sacked out just as soon as we'd thawed out and had something to eat. Now this is the strange bit." Doug settled back on the bed and his voice dropped. "I woke up real early next morning. No snow still, but cold enough to freeze your butt off. I crawled out and I could still see the stars, but it was getting light."

"Yeah, yeah."

"I'm getting to it. This is important. I looked out and I just knew it was my day. That out there a deer was waiting for me. Crazy, huh? So I got dressed without waking Dad and went back to the same place."

"Was that old squirrel there?"

"Nope. It was quiet. Quieter than you could believe. I hid there, hardly breathing, getting colder and colder. After a time I began to wonder what the hell I was doing there, when I could have been back in my warm sleeping bag. But I hung on. And it got lighter. Almost sunrise. My butt was frozen and I couldn't feel my legs. I was just thinking that I was going to have to move before I froze to death, when ...," he paused dramatically.

"Go on."

"My deer strolled by, casual as could be."

Mike shivered. "Could you see it clear?"

"Not at first. Just a movement. Grey and brown, you know, like the trees. It was an ear twitching. A muley, all right. So I'm staring through my rifle scope by now, and blinking because my eyes keep watering. And the head comes up and

I see those antlers. Oh, man! So there I am, not moving a muscle. And there he is, not alarmed, you know, but twitchy, ready to go. So I aim below the shoulder, and take a good breath, let it out real slow and squeeze off. Man, what a feeling!"

"A clean shot first time?"

"Didn't even nick a rib. It keeled right over, and I'm charging through the bush to get to it, you know. Then I hear this awful noise, like a grizzly breaking through the brush. And I think: No way I'm going to leave my deer for some old bear. So I'm standing over it, with my rifle cocked and aimed, and what should come bursting out the bushes ... ?"

"Not a bear?"

"Uh-uh. Dad! And he yells: 'Don't shoot, you ape. It's me!' So I ease on the safety and put the gun down, and Dad grabs hold of me and starts hugging me and thumping my back and measuring those antlers and thumping me again. We must have made one hell of a noise! Then when we'd calmed down a bit we hauled it back to camp and skinned it out and butchered it. You know, it was a great feeling handing all that meat over to Mom. We're still eating deer steaks and hamburgers."

"What about the rest of the hide?"

"Had it tanned. Enough there for a pair of knee-high moccasins."

"You lucky bastard."

"I know it."

When Doug had gone, Mike lay in bed with his arms behind his head and imagined what it would be like seeing his deer, it would be a whitetail – he didn't want to copy Doug in everything – through the sights of his beautiful new rifle. But what was the use of dreaming? Even if he were better by next November the parents would never allow Mr. O'Reilly to take him hunting, even if Doug's dad were willing to take the responsibility of having him along.

But he lay and dreamed anyway about his own special hunt. Maybe he should go by himself, just sneak away from everyone, and wouldn't they be surprised when he came to town with a fine set of antlers. But it would be more fun if Doug were along. He'd need him to help skin out his deer.

—

It was a good dream and he went over it carefully, not rushing but filling in all the details he could from his own knowledge of the bush and what he'd heard from Doug and the members of the Gun Club. The dream helped to push away the dark, and eventually he fell asleep and slept clean through the night until breakfast next morning, which was some sort of a record.

But the rest of the day was no good at all. His white count was too high. The new treatment just wasn't getting the results it should. Dr. Gage looked disappointed, though he talked cheerfully about a new approach.

He tried to get Mother and Dad to talk about the new treatment that evening. "Did Dr. Gage tell you what he was going to try next?"

"He mentioned it." Dad rocked from foot to foot and

fidgeted with the bed-table.

"I don't know what they'll do if this one doesn't work." Mike voiced the fear that had been a weight on his chest all day.

"It'll work. He's a good man, Mikey." Mother put her hand over his. It felt good. Talk to me, he wanted to say. Please, Mom.

"For God's sake, George, stop fidgeting like that," she suddenly snapped. They both stared at her. She looked stricken. "I'm sorry. I didn't mean ..." Her lips trembled. She tightened them and smiled. Patted Mike's hand. But the safe feeling had gone, and in the silence that followed the dark began to come back.

Desperately Mike began to tell them about Doug's visit, about the trophy head, anything to fill the silence.

"... and next November I want to go after a whitetail. A real winner. Wouldn't it be great, Dad, if you could take some time off and come with me and the O'Reillys. You'd love it, I'm sure you would."

"Oh, Mike!" Mother's voice trembled. Then she laughed and went on. "You guys and hunting ..."

"Mom, honestly! Well, how about it, Dad? Wouldn't it be great?"

"Sure." Mike could tell he wasn't even listening. "What's this about Doug visiting you? You're only supposed to see family, you know."

"Doug pretty near is family, isn't he?" Mike managed a smile.

The new treatment was started the next morning. It was even worse than the other. The sight of his food tray made him vomit. By evening his temperature was climbing and his bones hurt as if they'd been pumped full of hot lead.

Dad and Mom stopped by for only a few minutes.

"Hello, darling. Dr. Gage says you're doing fine."

"Hang in there, son."

But their faces gave them away. They didn't really expect him to live, he could see that. Did he want to himself? Was it worth the pain? He wanted to scream at Dr. Gage, at the nurses, at everyone, to leave him in peace, to let him ...

That night the dark was worse than it had ever been. It crept up on him and savaged him like a bear at a deer's throat. He lay still with his fists clenched and when at last the fear got so bad that he couldn't stand it any more he crawled out of bed and staggered into the whiteness of the hospital corridor, where it was never night.

There was a phone in a niche not far from his door. He leaned against the wall and dialled Doug's number. He didn't have a watch, but it must have been awfully late. The phone rang and rang. When he finally heard Doug's voice it sounded half asleep.

"Huh?"

"Doug, it's me ... Mike."

"Mike!" The voice went up, and then dropped to a whisper. "Mike, what's the matter? Do you know what time it is?"

"No. Did I get you up? I'm sorry. I couldn't sleep. I just had to talk to someone...." All of a sudden there were no words for the way he felt. His chest and throat felt full and tight, and then he began to cry, leaning against the wall by the phone.

He could hear Doug's voice. "Mike, Mike, what's the matter?" but he couldn't answer. He put the phone down and stumbled along the corridor to his own room where the night nurse caught him, gave him a scolding and a drink of water and a pill that zonked him out for the rest of the night.

Next day the treatment was as bad as the day before, only this time Mike knew what to expect. If anything that made it worse. The day passed like a long bad dream, and when evening came he felt as if he were a long long way from the real world.

Mother and Dad were like ghosts. They sat by his bed and looked at him and talked. But the things they said didn't seem to make any sense.

"Where's Doug? I want to see Doug." Doug was real. They couldn't turn him into a ghost, could they?

But Doug wasn't coming. Exams, Dad said. Studying for exams. Had Dad really said that? Doug would never let a little thing like an exam get in the way. "Tell him I want to see him. Please. It's important ..."

He must have closed his eyes or drifted off for a minute, because when he opened them again the room was empty and someone had drawn the drapes across the windows, shutting out the night. His head was clear again and he could think properly. He switched on the reading light and looked at the clock above the door. Only seven. Good. Visiting hours weren't over yet. Doug would come soon.

He lay in the pool of light that the reading lamp made above his bed. It was like a small white island in a sea of dark. A desert island....

He watched the door. Footsteps came close and he propped himself up on one elbow. His head was swimmy. The steps went on by. Oh well, plenty of time yet. The second hand jerked around the white face. Round and round. Nearly eight. Maybe Doug had missed the earlier bus. The stupid jerk was always missing buses. No sense of time.

The door banged open, but it was only a ward aide with a trolley laden with juice and milk. Mike's welcoming smile faded. "But you don't come till visiting hours are over," he told her.

"Right." She looked up at the clock. "Eight-oh-one. What'll you have? Apple juice, lemonade, Sprite ...?"

He shook his head and she went out again. The door of his prison swung to with a thump. That's what it was. Prison. He lay back and stretched the cramped arm he'd been leaning on. How skinny his wrist looked. Not as if it belonged to him at all. It didn't really. It belonged to the hospital. All of him belonged to the hospital and they could do what they wanted with him. The plastic tag on his arm said that. He wouldn't be free until it came off again.

Why hadn't Doug come? Dad hadn't allowed it. The answer jumped into his mind. Bingo! He knew it was right. And there wasn't a thing he could do about it.

The night nurse came in to settle him and he challenged her. "I asked for Doug. For my friend. Why didn't he come?"

She went back to the station to check for him. "Family only, it says," she told him.

"Who said?" He struggled up in bed. "Dr. Gage or my father? I bet it was my father."

"I don't know, I'm afraid." She turned off his light and left him with the dark.

Mike lay and thought about being in prison. His anger kept the dark at bay. When the night nurse came in hours later to check on him he kept his eyes shut, so that she thought he was sleeping. After she had gone he opened his eyes again and outstared the dark. Thinking.

He didn't get breakfast before treatment. Just a drink and some pills that were supposed to stop the nausea. He wouldn't take them.

"But you have to." The student nurse was flustered. "They're on your chart." He just shook his head.

A little later Miss MacGillivary rustled in. She was the RN and she was one grim lady. "What's all this nonsense, Michael?"

"No nonsense. I've decided not to go on with the treatment. That's all."

"Silly boy. You want to get well, don't you?"

"Guaranteed?" He gave her a hard look. You can fight the system, he thought, and felt good.

She looked squarely back at him. "You know there are no guarantees. But we do our best." Not a bad old trout, really.

"I know. It's not you. But I've been thinking, and I've decided it's not worth it."

"Giving up? A big boy like you?"

"Right." He outstared her, calling her bluff.

"I'll have to phone Dr. Gage about this."

"Yeah." He'd won the first round.

About nine o'clock Jim Gage came in and sat down on the end of Mike's bed. "What's the game?" He pinched Mike's toes.

"I don't know what you mean." Mike pulled his feet out of the way.

"Oh, come on. You're so hot on the truth. It's a two-way street, isn't it? You're not a quitter. What are you really up to?"

"I need to see Doug. I phoned him last ... no, the night before. I was sure he'd come. Did you stop him?"

Jim Gage shook his head.

"Then it was Dad and Mother. I knew it! Why do they do this to me?"

"Hey, come on. You know they love you."

"Damn funny way of showing it." Mike's mouth went crooked. He swallowed and blinked. "Why do they hate Doug?"

"Hate? Oh, Mike, try and keep your perspective. They don't hate him. Look, you must realize that your parents are scared to death for you. Their only concern is to protect you."

"They're sure I'm going to die, aren't they?" Mike looked hard at the doctor.

He looked back, his hazel eyes clear and honest. "Yes, they are. And it doesn't mean you're going to, either. Some parents, not a lot but some, can't and won't believe that *their* child has leukemia. Then when the facts get in the way so completely that their delusion is destroyed they swing to the opposite extreme. It doesn't mean they don't love you. On the contrary. They just won't allow themselves to hope in case their hope is disappointed."

Mike found he was sweating. He wiped a hand over his face. "Funny way to love," he said again.

"Sure. People are funny. Part of growing up is accepting that. Making allowances."

Mike nodded. "Okay. But I have to see Doug. He's in the real world. And I want to get back there, you know?"

"Hey." Jim Gage's hand was over his, firm and warm. "It's all right. I understand. I'm on your side. So long as there's no danger of infection I think you're better off seeing people."

"But the parents knew best." Mike managed a grin.

Jim Gage nodded.

"All right." Mike felt awfully tired, but it was going to work out. "I refuse treatment unless Doug's allowed to visit me."

"You're still a minor. Your parents could insist ..."

"I may look as if I've just been through the wringer, but I'd still put up one hell of a fight."

Jim Gage stood up, smiling. "I bet you would. Don't worry. I'll phone them."

—

Dad arrived an hour later. "Mike, what do you think you're doing? Have you any idea how much you've upset your mother?"

Don't make me feel guilty, Mike thought. Don't use Mother as a weapon. Be strong, Dad, please. I need your strength. Aloud he said, "I'm sorry. But I have to do this."

"Why? You've got to take the treatment." Dad moved closer, close enough to touch. "Without it you haven't a chance. You'll …" He stopped. Truth trembled as fragile as a spider's web between them. Mike reached out a hand, touched Dad's.

"Without it I'll die. That's not so hard to say, is it, Dad?"

"Oh, dear God." Dad got up. Walked to the window. Stared out.

"Dad, please."

"What is it, son?" He turned, a dark silhouette against the light. A familiar shape, but faceless.

"I need Doug."

"He's not good for you. He overexcites you, fills you up with impossible dreams."

"With hope."

"Not us? Not your parents?"

"I'm sorry, Dad," he whispered. "You've got no hope to give me."

Dad turned his back again, beating on the heat register with his plump clean office hands. "Suppose we permit Doug to visit you, will you go on with the treatment?"

"Yes." Mike's voice cracked. His lips were very dry.

"All right. I'll see to it." He came back and stood at the foot of the bed. "But … Mike, when your mother comes to see you, don't let her know … the way you feel about us."

He looked smaller, suddenly, like a balloon that had shrunk.

The door swung shut. Victory.

Mike turned and buried his face in the pillow. He never knew victory would taste so bitter.

—

Doug came to see him that evening. He tiptoed in, awkward and red about the ears. "Hey, how are you?"

"The better for seeing your ugly mug."

"I was going to come before, but they said no visitors. That phone call the other night ..."

"Yeah."

"Scared the hell out of me."

"Sorry. I was a bit out of my tree, I guess."

"I thought maybe it was something like that. Drugs are funny." He sat down in the chair by the bed, smiling, but not his usual talkative self.

Mike didn't mind. It was good just to have him there. Behind him the clock above the door seemed to be gobbling up the minutes. Usually it dragged. "There's so little time," he blurted out.

Doug followed his eyes and looked up at the clock. "Sorry. Hockey practice. I'll be in earlier tomorrow."

"I didn't mean that. I meant ... living time."

"You mean ... like, for the things you want to do?"

"Yeah. And the things I don't even know I want yet. It's not fair. It's like being scratched from the team even before the try-outs."

Doug cleared his throat. "You sound pretty down. Do they ... *say* you're going to die?"

"No. But it isn't going that good."

Doug turned red and kicked the bed leg. "You know, for what it's worth, you're the ... best friend I've ever had...."

"Thanks. But it's not enough. Shit, I'm sixteen and right on, you know, the edge of it all. What have I done so far? I've never owned a car. I've never brought home a trophy head.... Mike Rankin did this, you know."

"Your father said I shouldn't have brought in that head. I didn't mean to upset you."

"You didn't. It helped. But I want it for me. And I want to know what it's like to ... to sleep with a girl. When I get really down, I think about my epitaph. Michael Rankin, aged sixteen. He never got to vote or drive a car and he died a virgin."

"So what d'you want me to do? Smuggle a girl in here?"

"Oh bug off!" Mike threw a pillow at him.

Doug put it behind his shoulders and stared at Mike. "Boy, you sure don't think much of yourself, do you?"

"Well, why should I?"

"Maybe you should think about what we think of you. People like me and Dad and Mom. The other kids. So we don't talk about it. Neither do you. But what you're doing right now is braver and more ... more important than hunting or car racing, or making out with a girl."

"What the hell are you talking about?"

"Dying, you idiot. Jeez, that's the big one. Living with the idea that maybe you're going to die."

"I don't have much choice about it."

"No. But the way you ... well ... face up to it, that's your choice. Isn't it?"

The cold truth at the end of the dark. Funny it should be Doug telling it....

Mike swallowed and tried to smile. "Do you know what I had to go through to get you in here?"

"No. Why?"

"I'm wondering why the hell I bothered."

"Oh." Doug thought about it. "Did I say something wrong?"

"Yes. No. Hell, I don't know."

"Want me to go?"

"No. I don't want ... oh, shit, it's time anyway. But you'll come back tomorrow, won't you?"

"Sure. I'll be here."

After he'd gone Mike lay and thought about what Doug had said. It was the coldest, most depressing thinking he'd ever done. If learning to die was what his life was supposed to be all about, then he was going to have to learn to face the dark, not try and run from it. He lay and wrestled with this idea until the night nurse caught him staring at the ceiling and gave him a pill that pushed back the dark for a while and let him sleep.

SEVEN

The fire burned fiercely, pushing back both the cold and the dark. As he looked up, his eyes following the flight of the sparks, Mike saw that it had stopped snowing. In a few minutes, as his eyes adjusted to the darkness above the fire, he was able to see the weak light of a few stars between the windtorn tatters of cloud. The storm had passed, and he had survived it.

He gathered together the remnants of his emergency kit, tucked his pant-legs into the tops of his boots, and stood up to kick out the fire. He emptied his gun and stowed the cartridges in his pocket. Even with the safety on he didn't want to struggle back to his camp through the dark and the drifting snow with a loaded gun.

He wasn't afraid of losing his way now. There was only one direction to go and that was downhill. That would lead him to the river sooner or later; and once he had found that, he only had to follow the river bank downstream to his camp. Thinking of the camp made him think of food, hot food. He realized just how empty he was, and tried to push the thought out of his mind and concentrate on getting there.

It was lucky that the way back was so simple, because if he had had to rely on landmarks he would have been hopelessly lost. The storm had totally changed the appearance of everything. The wind had sculptured the snow into fantastic shapes that disguised the terrain beneath, and elsewhere it had scoured right down to the ground so that the frozen grass and small saplings were exposed.

It was a long time before Mike reached the river. Even though he made detours around recognizable drifts he still got trapped occasionally and found himself floundering knee-deep in soft snow. His one fear was of breaking or twisting an ankle between branches or stones hidden under the deceptive smoothness of the wind-polished snow. It was midnight by the time he finally reached camp, and the stars were blazing down out of a sky veiled with only small shreds of cloud.

Even his camp was unfamiliar, and at first he nearly walked right past it. Was that strange humped shape sagging under a burden of snow really his tent? He brushed away the snow with finicky care and tightened the guy-ropes. It had been a heavy load, but nothing was broken or damaged.

He used the frying pan to shovel out the fireplace and pushed the snow well out of the way. There were no trees directly above, so he had no fear of being disconcerted by another wet avalanche. It was a luxury to make a fire with the dry wood he had stored inside the tent, and as many matches as he needed. He'd never thought what a miracle a match was until he'd been without them.

He lit the fire and opened a big can of stew. Waited, staring into the flames, while it heated. When at last it bubbled he took it off the fire and ate it with a spoon, right out of the pan, burning his tongue on the pieces of potato and carrot. Why did the vegetables always get red-hot when the meal and gravy were just right, he wondered. He scraped the bottom of the pan and then mopped up the remains of the gravy with a piece of bread, polishing around the inside of the pan for every last drop. It wasn't the gourmet meal he had planned while he was sitting out the storm. It was better, far better.

Warm, his stomach marvellously full, he shucked off his outer clothes and crawled into his sleeping bag. He didn't bother to make up the fire. He didn't even think about his enemy, the dark. His eyes closed and he slid instantly down a long chute into sleep. Outside the tent the fire glowed rosily for a time. The last log caved into the ashes, sending up a shower of golden sparks. The glow faded, and the dark spread its own kind of comfort over the camp.

Mike woke before sunrise from a dream in which he had stalked a deer as white as a unicorn, with many-branched antlers. He woke with a sense of accomplishment. For the first time in months he had slept right through the night untroubled.

He woke too with another sense, that seemed to have something to do with his dream, that everything was moving the way it was supposed to, and that today, without any shadow of doubt in his mind, he was going to bag his trophy whitetail.

He made the fire, went to the river to wash and get water for coffee and hot cereal. The ice had grown out an arm's length from the bank, but only cat-ice, not safe to walk on. He had to break through it with the side of the saucepan before he could get at the water. He looked up as he walked back. The sky was dark above, but there was a tinge of colour in the southeast. His breath rose in great clouds in the still air.

He ate a big breakfast, and when he'd tidied away the remains, he made a couple of sandwiches and tucked them in the inside pocket of his downfill where they wouldn't freeze. Carefully he replenished the emergency kit. He would never forget to take it with him now.

One last look around, almost a ceremony. His camp had already acquired a homey look, as if he had been there for a long time, had established a right to that small patch of wilderness. He extinguished the fire carefully and fastened the outer tent flap. Everything neat and tidy, as it should be. From the big spruce to the southeast the whisky-jacks screamed at him, scolding him for leaving them nothing to eat.

Soft-footed through the snow Mike set off uphill towards the fire road. As he walked he ran through in his mind everything he knew about whitetail deer, and thought about his whitetail and how he was going to bag it. To have a large enough spread of antlers to score as a trophy head a deer must have lived at least four years and be smarter than most, to have avoided hunters, grizzlies and wolves for all of its life. And even a stupid whitetail had so much going for it, it was a wonder that anyone managed to bag them.

His whitetail could hear a fingernail click at seventy metres. It could see a man's hand move at two hundred and fifty metres; and its sense of smell was so acute that it would be instantly aware of Mike's presence, if the wind or thermal currents favoured it, long before Mike was within shooting range.

Even if Mike got on its tail the whitetail could run for kilometres at the speed of a city car, and jump as far as thirty metres downhill if it had to. It sounded depressing, when all that Mike had going for himself was a pair of not particularly acute ears, eyes that could be augmented by a 4X scope, no great stamina or speed, and not much sense of smell at all beyond being able to recognize bacon and coffee in the morning. But Mike wasn't depressed. The challenge elated him. He remembered what Doug's dad had told them. "Your deer's got a natural instinct for survival way past any man on earth, except possibly an Inuit or an Australian aborigine. But he's all instinct and no brain. Don't forget that. It'll give you the edge.

"A whitetail born in the Swan Hills will want to stay put in the Swan Hills. In fact he'll stay as much as possible within a kilometre or so of the place where he was born. You've got no ears or eyes or nose to speak of, but you've got two really big advantages. You've got a brain and you've got an imagination. Use them both. Think yourself into the skin of your deer and you've got it made."

Mike tried to think himself into the skin of a deer and at the same time remember everything he'd read. In winter time there was little browse among the dense trees that covered the Swan Hills like a dark blanket. They needed the sort of vegetation that grew up in open spaces, away from the light – and moisture – stealing pines and spruces.

Before man came that meant areas burned out by natural crossfire. Now man had put his hand on the wilderness and crossed it with seismic cuts and fire roads. As soon as the big trees were removed grasses, wildflowers, Saskatoon and rose bushes, and the tender saplings of aspen sprang up in their place. Even in the winter, even under fifty centimetres of snow, there was still enough to support the small herds of deer, both whitetail and muley, that roamed the Swan Hills.

But it would take them time to get enough browse to fill themselves, especially after a storm like last night's, and they would likely stay past sunrise, so long as they felt safe. Mike walked quickly and quietly under the dark trees while the stars slowly faded out and the light in the southeast began to strengthen.

He came across a runway dotted with the fresh hoof-prints of several deer. The snow softly blanketed the leaves and cushioned his footsteps. He followed the runway uphill towards the fire cut, treading carefully, not allowing his clothes to brush against the low branches that overhung the deer's path. He stopped every ten steps or so to look around, to listen with his human ears that could hear nothing but the sound of his heart pounding, to smell nothing but the clean, early-morning snowy absence of smell.

He was getting close to the cut. The trees were thinning out and spindly aspen were replacing the great rough trunks of pine and spruce. There were shadows too now, running long across the ground ahead of him like wide shallow stairs. It was dawn.

He stood in the shadow of a large poplar near the open ground of the cut and scanned carefully ahead of him. Nothing. Cautiously he moved closer to the cut. In another minute he would be able to see along it in both directions as far as the rolling terrain would allow. But when he stepped out from cover, the deer, if they were there, would also see him. He moved with patient caution, moving quietly a step or two forward, stopping, looking around, trying to think like a deer, act like a deer, which would stop to browse, to check its back trail, and then move on....

Within the frail shelter of the spindly aspen that edged the cut Mike looked out. The snow shone so brilliantly after the deep shadows beneath the trees that his eyes smarted. He squeezed them shut and then squinted between the lids, looking along the cut to the north.

He blinked and squinted again. There they were! Right out in the open, so clearly silhouetted against the snow that he couldn't believe they were real. He'd been right. The heavy snow had made the search for browse more difficult. Although the sun was now rising, flooding the southeastern sky with light and sending long shadows rippling blue across the snow, the deer were still there right out in the open, pawing away the snow with their hooves, bending their heads to eat, raising them frequently to look around.

It was going to be difficult. With three of them bunched together it seemed that one always had his head up, on guard. Very, very slowly Mike lifted his rifle and sighted down the scope. At least there wasn't enough light yet to flash on the glass and warn them. They jumped into focus: three bucks. One of them was a young fellow with only three points to an antler including the brow tines which were hardly more than knobs. The second was a good-sized buck, a four-pointer with long tines, thick neck and shoulders. The kind he'd feel proud to bag any time. Any time, except after seeing the third buck.

After the third buck there was no other whitetail in the whole of Swan Hills. At the sight of it Mike's heart began to pound and his throat felt thick and hot with excitement. The third buck stood taller by almost a hand than the second, and its massive neck supported the biggest rack that Mike had seen in any film or photo. It was a five-pointer, the tines long and clean, the rack well-balanced, the brow tint almost as long as the antler tines.

It lifted its head and stared, almost insolently, towards Mike. Mike could see the royal sweep of the antlers, the great curve outward and forward, as the buck stared at him face on. There must have been more than half a metre between the two halves of the curve. He held his breath. The buck continued to stare in his direction instead of going back to browsing. Had it seen him? More than a hundred metres separated them. Was it possible that the deer had scented him? But there was no breeze and the air was still too cool for thermals to have developed.

The other bucks browsed on, pulling at the long grass under the snow, filling their stomachs quickly before the full light of the day sent them to seek shelter among the trees, to find a hiding place where they might lie and ruminate until evening. Regularly the young one and the four-pointer flicked up their heads, looked, listened, scented the air, and regularly ducked down to eat again. Still the big fellow stared in Mike's direction.

Mike didn't move a hair. I'm not here, he told the buck in his mind. Go on, stupid, eat. There's no one here. The buck still stared. The rifle became heavier and heavier, and Mike could feel his hands wanting to tremble. The palms were sweating. He wouldn't even let himself blink. He was breathing only into the top centimetre or so of his lungs. If only the big one would look away, just for a second, so that Mike could ease down the bolt of his rifle. But what about the noise of the bolt? Would he have time to squeeze off that one perfect shot?

Something was going on in the big buck's mind. It snorted suddenly. The sound travelled incredibly clearly on the cold still air. The other two heads came up as if they'd been pulled by strings. The old fellow snorted again. It turned away, showing its white tail, carried erect against his rump like a white banner. The others turned, tails up too, and without haste or panic melted into the trees on the far side of the cut.

As soon as he heard the second snort Mike had pulled back the bolt on his rifle, pushed it forward and down. His finger was on the trigger, the rifle at his shoulder. For one heartstopping instant he had the big one caught in the cross-hairs of his sight. Then as he moved the rifle in the direction of their flight there was nothing but a tangle of branches, a tree trunk, more brush.

He lowered the gun and raised the bolt handle. For an instant he was flooded with sick disappointment. So close! Then he told himself not to be a fool. After all, it was something even to have seen one of the big ones. That was something in itself, especially for a novice like him. It would have been almost too easy, too demeaning to the great buck, if he had been able to down him with his very first shot of the season.

I've got all day, he told himself. If not today, there's always tomorrow. Or the next day. Every day until the season's over. I can find out where he beds during the day and at night. I can follow the runways he likes to take. I can find out where he drinks. I'll get him, and no other, Mike vowed. He's mine.

The snowstorm that had nearly ended Mike's life was now his ally. Printed in the fresh carpet of snow he would be able to see every move that the five-pointer made, if he had the eyes for it, and the stamina, and the patience to hang well back and remember to walk and think like a deer.

Mike walked out onto the deserted fire road. The sun was full up now, and the long white ribbon unrolled from left to right, straight and spotless. But in places the wind had blown the snow into soft scalloped drifts with trailing edges that held the last dawn shadows.

Once he had plunged unexpectedly up to his knees and floundered wetly about before he could get a footing again, Mike learned to watch out for these shadowy trails. He brushed the snow carefully off his jeans. Wet cotton would be a misery to walk in, and might freeze up before it had a chance to dry. His rifle was all right. He'd automatically held it above his head as he'd stumbled forward into the drift.

Lurking in the brush at the edge of the cut he had guessed that he'd been about a hundred metres from the browsing deer. As he detoured from drift to drift he began to think that he'd badly underestimated the distance. Range was tricky to guess out here; the air was so still and so clear that the only thing that stopped you seeing forever was the curve of the distant hills cutting the sky.

Down the centre of the cut was a long, wind-scoured swathe where the dried grass was exposed. This had been the deer's feeding ground, the reason he had found the three bucks together, although he knew that normally whitetails tended to be solitary. He walked along carefully, watching the ground trampled by the sharp heart-shaped hooves. Wasn't it just about there that the big fellow had been grazing when it had looked up and seen him? The small one had been over on the right and the other buck a bit to the left....

The hoofprints were a muddle where the three bucks

had moved to and fro, pawing away the light snow cover and tugging at the grass below. But behind the feeding area there were three clear sets of tracks where the snow deepened. If he could pick out the five-pointer's tracks and stay glued to them ...

It seemed to Mike that the central set of prints were the deepest and perhaps a bit larger. In his mind's eye was the clear picture of the rumps of the three deer vanishing into the bush, big white tails feathering up. The biggest tail in the centre. He made up his mind and followed the central line of tracks across the cut.

At the forest's edge he stopped. From now on he'd be in new country. He was beyond the fire road, beyond the valley of the Freeman River. Getting back would no longer simply be a matter of heading downhill until he hit the river and then following it downstream until he came to his camp. From now on he would have to pay attention to where he was going, because if he happened to get badly turned around he might find another fire road or seismic cut and get so muddled that he would never find his way out.

He turned and took a bearing of the direction of his camp. Pretty nearly due east. Now all he had to do was to keep track of whether he was moving in a generally north or south direction as he followed the buck west, so that he could count on getting back to this cut if he returned due east. Then he'd be on familiar territory and could find the river again.

He stowed away the compass in the breast pocket of his

mackinaw, tucked the rifle comfortably under his arm and stepped into the shadows of the trees, back into the dawn chill that still lingered beneath the branches away from the warmth of the sun.

Here were the big one's hoofprints all right. No doubt about it. The buck hadn't even been scared. Its tail had gone up, but it hadn't laid its ears back and it hadn't leapt into the brush; really, it had been more like a stroll. That was good news; it meant that probably it would head straight for its favourite day-time bedding spot close to one of the main runways.

Mike stood still and told himself to be patient. Hurry could ruin everything at this stage. He let his eyes grow accustomed to the shadows ... it had really been painfully bright out there on the open cut. His heart was pounding and a heady excitement made him feel more alive than he'd felt in a year. But the excitement was all in his blood and his guts, and his brain was icy calm.

He knew that if he charged after the buck it would be off and running, and with no hunter friend to head it off and turn it back towards him he could kiss his chance of a trophy head goodbye. Give it plenty of time to bed down, he told himself. Soon the sun will be high enough to warm the ground a little through the trees. The buck will settle down then and start to ruminate, like a cow lying down to chew its cud on a lazy summer's afternoon.

He stood very still and tried to ignore the cold that began to creep up his legs. His eyes were slowly adjusting.

Now he could see the buck's prints clearly. A few metres ahead of him was a place where it had leapt over a tangled mass of deadfall. He'd have to go around that or he'd disturb every living thing in the bush. He bet that beyond the deadfall there'd be a runway. Whitetails were creatures of habit, he reminded himself. They kept to the same resting and feeding areas, the same drinking spots.

He moved cautiously along the deadfall to his left, walking half a dozen steps, looking around, trying to distinguish between ordinary light and shade of tree trunk and branch, and something different, something that was neither tree nor bush. It took him a slow fifteen minutes to work his way around the tangle of deadfall that the buck must have leapt in a single graceful bound.

His patience paid off. Beyond the tangle of fallen trees and broken branches was a runway. And once again the snowstorm proved to be a blessing. He did not have to distinguish between the hoofprints of numerous bucks and does made over many days. The snow lay about ten centimetres deep in the areas where it had not drifted, and its smoothness was broken only by the deer that had passed up and down it in the course of this one dawn's feeding.

There were other tracks, of course. The distinctive large rear and tiny front paws of a snowshoe hare, the small friskinesses of squirrels on some late food-gathering trip; and there were bird prints, minute half-opened fans that barely broke the surface of the snow.

Mike felt every sense grow keener. He was seeing as he

had never seen before. His hearing was so acutely tuned that when his arm brushed a dead branch the faint whisper of wood against nylon made his heart jump.

He moved cautiously along the runway. Level with the tangle of deadfall he found the set of prints where the big five-pointer had landed. There was a tiny spurt of snow beyond the prints which gave a notion of its speed as it had jumped. Then it had stopped. There was a neat pile of droppings. Obviously it had looked around, seen nothing to alarm it and then trotted off downhill along the runway.

With finicky care Mike followed. He walked no more than half a dozen steps at a time. He stopped, looked ahead, to left and right, his senses tuned to a finer pitch than he had known them to be capable of. It was like being high. Mike had only smoked up once, and he felt like that time now, only this was a thousand times better. He felt not so much that he was floating away from his body, but that he and his body were floating along together. He felt light and yet in control. His feet went precisely where he told them to. He was breathing evenly, without strain, and his heart no longer pounded.

It was so quiet that he felt as if he might be the last man on earth. When the high whine of a jet engine came piercing down through the trees and he looked up and saw the contrail bisecting the clear sky, he realized with a shock that it was just the ordinary morning flight up to Grande Prairie and the Peace, with ordinary people aboard sitting three abreast with their briefcases and shopping bags, not knowing that in the forest below he, Mike Rankin, was looking up at them.

After it had gone he waited, quiet within himself, until the stillness came flooding back into the forest. Only then did he move. Six steps. Pause. Look. It was much more tiring than walking briskly.

But it was the only way. Even on the snow carpet there were tiny noises when he moved. He couldn't completely cancel out his physical presence. But he could act like an animal instead of a man. Man was always in a hurry. Always on the way from somewhere to somewhere else. The shortest distance between two points is a straight line – to a man. To an animal there is no real destination, just a present leading slowly towards another present.

So Mike walked and stopped, as if he was browsing. Then he ambled on again. And watched the shadows all the time. The ambiguous patterns of light and shade. He watched for a roundness that did not belong in the angularity of the trees. He watched for a twitching ear in the still brush.

And it worked. He had been moving down the runway for perhaps half an hour, maybe longer, when he saw a curve of light over to the left. Off the path, but not far off it. With breathless care he drew back into the shelter of a tree trunk, untucked his rifle from his armpit and raised it slowly to his shoulder.

He looked through the scope. Where was it? Had he imagined something? A tangle of branches, seeming so close to his face that he flinched, swept across the scope as he slowly moved the rifle. There! Wasn't that it? A grey curve of rump in the circle of the scope. But was it his buck? Was it a buck at all?

He stood motionless, and then moved the rifle just a whisker to the right, so that when the head did come up again, he'd see it clearly. Come on. Time to stop browsing and look around. Come on!

At last the head did come up, and his heart plunged in disappointment. The head was antlerless. He glassed carefully around the whole area in case there was a buck close by, but he could see nothing else.

Damn! If he went on down this runway he was bound to disturb the doe, and if she jumped up and went crashing through the brush the noise would alert every other deer around. Was there any way he could get past without her noticing? On all fours perhaps? But he'd probably make even more noise that way and spook her regardless.

The only answer was to backtrack until he found another runway that would bypass the place where the doe was bedded. Then he could get back onto *this* runway, pick up his buck's trail again, and head on downwards towards the valley.

He turned back the way he had come, remembering to walk in the rhythm he had established already, walk, pause, walk, pause. Luckily he didn't have to backtrack too far before he came on another runway heading in approximately the same direction, but farther up the slope. He followed it patiently and with extra caution until he was sure he was well past the place where he had spotted the resting doe.

When a trail crisscrossed his, he turned down it to the

left, and when he came across another one more or less parallel to the slope of the hill he stopped and stared down at the snowy surface. Were his buck's prints among those marked in the snow? He should know them on sight – he'd stared at them long enough. But there was a real mess of hoofprints right at the intersection of the trails; it was hard to tell. In the end he went a few metres back. There they were! Heavier and larger by far than any of the others. He was back on the right track.

Mike felt a terrible impulse to charge along at top speed to make up for lost time. He pulled himself up short. He was beginning to think like a man again. To a deer there was no such thing as "lost time." Time had no real meaning at all. There was only light and dark. Warm and cold. Hungry or satisfied. Thirsty or slaked....

Casually, with no hurry in the world, he drifted on down the runway, on the way to that moment in his destiny that he felt he'd been waiting for all his life.

EIGHT

Not just to bag any deer, but a trophy.... The seed of the idea had been planted that evening in March when Doug lugged that great unwieldy mule deer head over to the hospital. At first dreaming about it was only a game to keep the dark at bay. But it was Doug who made it real. It was Doug who wouldn't let him give up on his dream. Faithful to his promise he came to visit Mike every evening, and one evening Mike shared the secret of his dream.

Doug gave a dismayed whistle. "From Swan Hills? I don't know if a trophy head's ever been taken from there. It's the climate and diet, you know, as well as the age ..."

"It was a stupid idea anyway," Mike muttered, wishing he'd kept quiet. "What chance have I got of getting any deer?"

"Hell, I don't know." Doug sat up abruptly. A little opposition always got him going. "If you want it badly enough you'll get it – maybe not a trophy, but a decent head."

"You think so?"

"You bet."

"I wonder if I could …" Mike put his hands behind his head and stared up at the ceiling. "Sometimes this thing's so close I can nearly touch it. It's more real than this place."

"You can do it."

"But then I think about Dad and Mother. I mean, they wouldn't even let me go on that skiing weekend to Jasper – remember? They'll never let me go hunting. No way."

"So, if they won't give you permission, then you'll just have to sneak off without telling them, won't you?"

Mike sat up and stared at him.

Doug went red. "I didn't say you should. I'm being logical, that's all. I guess it depends on how important it is."

"How …?" Mike stopped. His brain began to tick over and excitement rushed up inside him, warm and lively. "Could I? I wonder if I could. Oh hell, how'd I get up there? I can't drive, even if I could get hold of a truck or something."

"I told you we were getting a pick-up. Dad takes delivery of it next month. I'll be able to use it, and you too. All you've got to do is get your licence."

"I could get lessons at the AMA."

"Sure, or I could teach you, if it came to that. The only thing is you've got to have your parent's signature before you take your test."

"I knew there'd be a catch." Mike slumped. "Shit, it's hopeless. They'll never."

"Boy, you quit easy! There's more than one way of skinning a rabbit."

"Whatever that's supposed to mean."

"No need to snarl. What I mean is we have to be crafty and find a way of getting your parents to want the same things you want."

"But ..."

"Look, don't worry about that part of it now. Concentrate on getting better and I'll come up with a list of things to do."

The following evening Mike was waiting with his eye on the clock when Doug came in grinning and waving a large piece of paper. It looked like a very long list, but Doug ran down it, his optimism unruffled.

"... then there's the tent, sleeping bag ... you've got that ... food. We can pick up supplies any time, freeze-dried stuff and cans. You can keep them at my place so no one will ask questions – I'll make another list for food."

"I'll make that list – you like beans too much."

"Nice and breezy. Okay, an axe I can lend you. A knife you've already got, right? And a backpack. Really, there's not too much else to do. The Big Game certificate and authorization stamps and tags won't be on sale till July anyway, and you can buy them at Woodward's. Five dollars for the certificate and five for each authorization."

"Only one," Mike said firmly. The dream was growing more real as Doug talked. "One male whitetail deer."

"Okay, then. And you've already got your rifle and permit. That's the end of things to get. Now things to do. The Gun Club won't be meeting again till the fall, but as soon as you're out of here we'll put in some practise on the range.

Just to get your eye in."

"I hope I haven't forgotten how."

"Nah, you never forget, it's like swimming or riding a bike."

"Then there's transportation. That's the hardest."

Doug dropped his lists on the bed and began to prowl around the room. "Look, I've been thinking. The simplest thing would be for me to drive, in Dad's pick-up."

"Yeah. But ..."

"What's wrong with that?"

"I dunno. Suppose something came up and you couldn't go at the last minute. I'd be stranded. Another year, Doug. I don't know if I've got another year. I don't even know about this one."

"That's true. But I'm not crazy about the idea of you going off alone."

"Neither am I. But I'd still like to be prepared. Just in case."

"Okay. So now we have to think up a strategy so your parents will let you take driving lessons." Doug stopped talking.

"What?"

"Shut up. I'm thinking." He began to laugh. "It's sneaky, but I bet it'll work."

"What is it, for crying out loud?"

"As soon as you're out of here you ask your dad if *he'll* give you driving lessons."

"He'll never have the time. He's really busy now he's vice-president."

"Don't worry about it. That's the strategy. He'll be flattered you asked, see. Then you act kind of let down and disappointed. After that you think of the AMA."

Mike sat up and thought about it. Then he chuckled. "It is sneaky. But you're right. It's worth a try."

"Trust Uncle Doug. I know human nature."

"So I learn to drive, get my licence and enough practise over the summer. Then something to drive ..."

"I told you I'd fix it so you get to borrow the pick-up."

"I couldn't ..."

"Don't be an ass. It's important, isn't it?"

"Suppose I got into an accident? Suppose I dinged it? What about the insurance?"

"You worry too much. Dad always carries second-party risk. Anyone can drive it, so long as they have a licence."

Mike thought about it. He picked up Doug's list off the bed and read it through again. He couldn't help grinning. "It might work."

"It's going to work. All you have to do is get out of here," Doug pointed out matter-of-factly. "I'll help take care of the rest."

Two mornings later Jim Gage came in to see Mike. He was smiling broadly. "Looking good," he said. "What have you been up to? Go on this way and I'm going to have to throw you out of here. Then the normal routine, weekly IVs and tests, same as before."

"And then remission?"

"I don't see why not. It looks very promising."

The good news wasn't a surprise to Mike. He knew. He felt different. Ever since Doug had taken over his dream and started to make it real, the darkness had retreated. Mike was beginning to feel that he was in charge again. Oh, now and then the helpless feeling of panic would sneak up on him when he wasn't expecting it; but he had a weapon against the dark now – a Weatherby Mark V .257 rifle with a twenty-four-inch barrel and a 4X Bushnell scope, and in the cross-hairs of the sight a trophy head that was a record breaker.

"I'm proud of you, Mike." Jim Gage dropped a hand lightly on his shoulder. "I can play around with combinations of drugs and try and second-guess this thing, but without a fighting attitude from you it's all up the spout. For a while back there I thought it was, I'll tell you that now. But not any more."

"I've got plans." Mike confided. "And I'm sick of this place. No offence – nothing personal!"

"Anything special, these plans?"

Mike shrugged, and then his mind began to work in a crafty way that Doug would have been proud of. "One thing I really want to do is learn to drive, maybe even have my own car before too long."

"Sounds like an excellent idea."

"Perhaps you could put in a plug for me with the parents. You know what they're like...."

Jim Gage laughed. "I'll work on them, I promise. And you go on working at getting out of here. I'm sick of the sight of you too – nothing personal!"

Mike was sprung from the hospital on the following Thursday, and by the end of the next week he'd actually talked Dad into letting him take driving lessons. It worked just the way Doug had said.

"Only if you pass your learner's exam," Dad had bluffed, and drove him over in person to take it. But Mike had had time to learn the provincial driving regulations by heart, so the exam was a snap, and he walked out waving the precious card and showed it to Dad, who was waiting in the car.

Mother insisted on picking him up from school and driving him over to the AMA for his lessons, so he wouldn't get too tired, but he didn't fuss about it, thankful he'd got his way so far.

He passed his driver's test first crack. It began to look as if the old Rankin luck was coming back.

Doug thumped him on the back when he saw the endorsed licence. "Knew you could do it. Now all you need is lots of practice in the pick-up."

"You won't tell your Dad what we're planning, will you?"

"God, no. He'd be on our side all right, but he'd still feel he'd have to tell your parents."

The new pick-up, a tan-coloured Toyota four-by, arrived just after Easter. Mr. O'Reilly let Doug and Mike try it out whenever he didn't need it himself. And he gave them lots of hints on handling the shifts in rough country, how to gear down in really steep places and just how to use the engine as a brake.

Mike felt a bit guilty at deceiving him, but he pushed that to the back of his mind and concentrated on the main plan. April passed, and in May Jim Gage gave him the news he'd been waiting for. Remission.

There was nothing more he wanted. He'd got it all. Only six months to go till November. He tore over to Doug's house....

Two days later he was watching an outdoors adventure program on TV when Dad called to him from the front yard.

"What is it, Dad?" The man was explaining about the fly he'd used on a seven-pound trout.

"Come out here, son. I've got something to show you."

Mike got up impatiently and went to the front door. There, parked in the driveway, was a neat little Celica, bright red with black upholstery. He stared. "You've bought a new car?" It really wasn't Dad's style. He went for the big ones with air conditioning and automatic everything. No fun to drive at all.

He ran down the front steps and walked around the car. Ran his hand lovingly over the paint job. Factory new. He poked his head through the window and looked at the dash.

Dad grabbed his hand and pushed the keys into it.

"What ...?" Mike stared. His name was engraved on the tag. "Jeez, d'you mean ...?"

"It's yours, son." Dad's face was red and smiling. "For you, anything."

Even in the middle of being stunned and loving the car with a passion and wanting to jump right in it and drive off at top speed, just to see what it would do, Mike felt rotten.

He felt guilty at the anger he had so often felt against Dad, and knowing that he'd feel that way again before very long. Then he felt doubly guilty at the way he was deceiving him about the hunting trip.

He'd like to have given the keys back, even while he was loving the car like mad, but how could he? His hands got sweatier and sweatier. He wiped them on his jeans and then opened the car door and slid into the driver's seat. After all, he couldn't stand there forever. The inside had that marvellous new car smell, metal and leather and plastic. He ran his eyes over the dash. Only forty kilometres on the odometer. There was a trip meter and even a tachometer....

He swallowed and slid the key into the ignition. Turned it. Just touched the gas pedal. It started like a bird. He looked up, and just for once knew exactly what would make Dad happy.

"Can I take you for a spin, Dad?"

Dad was grinning broadly. "You bet, son."

Mike eased the car down the driveway and turned right along the crescent. The streets had been swept clean of all the winter grunginess, the sand and dirt, lost overshoes and single mittens. The crabapples were bursting with white and red flowers, and there were tulips, red-and-yellow striped, in the garden next door.

He drove with conscious care, watching all the traffic signals, remembering to shoulder check whenever he had to change lanes. Part of his mind was concentrating on impressing Dad. The other part was just bubbling with joy and pride at the performance of the Celica. His very own brand-new car....

They got onto the Yellowhead, and now he could relax a little. "Dad, thanks, it's great. It's the best thing that's ever happened to me."

"I'm glad." Dad's voice was different ... a bit less sure of himself. "You ... you mean such a lot to me, son, and it's so damn hard to tell you – y'know?"

Mike blinked and swallowed hard, concentrated on the road. "Yeah. It's the same with me, I guess. You know what I read the other day? People need four hugs a day just to keep going. Did you know that? Maybe ... "

Dad laughed, kind of choked up. "I'm out of practise. And you were so prickly there for a while ..."

"I know. I was a jerk. A bit mixed up and ... and mad. Know what I mean?"

"Yeah. Us too. We didn't handle it the best. Dr. Gage told us that. Made me kind of angry, him telling us about loving our own son. Afterwards I saw what he meant. But it's difficult to change your way of thinking when you get to my age."

"You're not that old, Dad."

"Don't you believe it, son."

Mike closed his eyes for a second and took a deep breath. His hands felt the power of the car as his foot touched the gas. The car chewed up the kilometres effortlessly.

"Hey, whoa there, Mike. Where are you off to, Alaska?"

Mike looked around and felt himself getting red. Without any conscious thought he'd turned off the

Yellowhead onto Highway 43, heading for Grande Prairie and Dawson Creek and, incidentally, for the turn-off that led to the Swan Hills.

He eased off the gas. He'd almost given away the whole plan. And yet ... maybe that wasn't such a bad idea. Dad had changed. He was trying to change more....

He checked the traffic, waited until the road was clear, and made a U-turn.

"You know, Dad," he said casually, "the thing I thought about most of all when I was in the hospital was the bush. I can't wait to get back to it. Sleeping in a tent, cooking over a fire, just goofing off ... I wish you could come too, some time...."

He glanced cautiously sideways. Dad was staring hard at the highway ahead. Mike saw the muscle beneath his jowl grow tense. Other than that his face didn't change. Real estate and poker – he was good at both. Good at not showing his feelings....

He spoke slowly. "I don't think camping's such a great idea. So many ways an accident can happen. Burns, axe wounds. I remember a man ..."

"Heck, things like that can happen anywhere to anyone. And as long as I'm in remission my blood's like anyone else's. I won't bleed to death or get a massive infection or anything like that." Dad didn't answer. "You don't expect me to spend the rest of my life wrapped in cotton batting, do you?" With a supreme effort he managed to keep his voice low and reasonable, though his knuckles went white as he clenched the wheel.

"Of course not, Mike. But you must see that there's more risk out in the bush than there is at home. I wouldn't want to go through that week in March again, you know that."

Neither would I, Mike thought. And I was the one who went through it, not you. Let me grow up. Be my friend, Dad, he wanted to say, but couldn't.

"You're holding that wheel far too tightly, son," Dad said.

"Right, Dad." He slackened off his grip and took a deep breath.

He felt relieved when the car was safely in the garage and the keys tossed on the bureau in his room. It was a super car, but he felt a twinge of guilt whenever he thought about the magnificence of the gift. But he was sixteen and a half, and he had to be free to do his own growing, in whatever time he'd got. The trophy head, hung on the wall of his room. With a brass plate with his name on it. Then they'd understand why he'd had to keep it a secret. He hoped they'd understand.

June seemed to pass in a flash, there was so much going on. Then, far too quickly, it was time for final exams. He did his best and made up his mind not to worry. There were more important things to worry about. Like going back to the hospital for tests. It was like sitting exams all over again. First the tight feeling of dread. Then the waiting. And then the phone call the following day. White count good. Platelets normal. Everything okay. Another tick mark against his future ... until the next set of tests.

He and Doug bought some of the supplies he'd need

and stowed them in a carton under Doug's bed where nobody'd ever look. They drove around town in the Celica. There were barbecues in the park and he and Doug got in some fishing, though Mother and Dad refused to let him stay away overnight so they couldn't go far enough north where the fish were really good.

Then, in the third week in July, he blew it. "I'm sorry, Mike," Jim Gage told him. "But you're going to have to come back in."

It's funny, thought Mike, his mind jumping all over the place as he hung onto the phone. All these months I've been dreading this phone call. Now it's come I don't believe it. Maybe it's a bad dream and in a minute I'll wake up. He shut his eyes and prayed: Let me be asleep. Don't let this be happening. Please.

When he opened his eyes again he was still leaning against the kitchen wall with the phone in his hand, and Jim Gage's voice, tinny and far off. He put the receiver back to his ear.

"Mike, are you all right?"

"Yes. Fine. It's okay." He pulled himself together. "Thanks for telling me yourself. When do you want me in?"

"Tomorrow will do. First thing. No breakfast," he warned.

"Right." Mike's mouth was dry. "Look, about the parents ..."

"I'll tell them. Don't worry. See you tomorrow."

"Sure."

He wandered out of the house and then got the Celica out of the garage. He'd go over to Doug's. Stay out of the way until Dr. Gage had had time to tell Mother and Dad. But when he got there Doug was out, taking his one-but-youngest sister to the dentist.

Mike got back into the car and drove out along the Yellowhead. He didn't take the turn north this time, but drove on west, fast, faster. The road was swallowed up under the wheels and the trees flashed by. Rolling fields. And then the trees closed in again. If only he could go far enough to escape the dark....

The bad curve by Carrot Creek was on him before he expected it and the car rocked and skidded. He geared down fast and got it back into control. He was sweating and breathing hard and his hands shook. He pulled over onto the shoulder. Jeez, that had been stupid. He didn't want to die.

He waited until the highway was clear and then turned and drove back to the city. He was hungry, he realized. He'd forgotten all about lunch.

Mother was trying not to cry when he came back into the house. She put her arms around him. "What did we do wrong? I must have let you get overtired, do too much ..."

"Mom, it's not your fault. It's no one's fault. Don't worry." *He* was comforting her.

August, September, October. Three months to go. I can do it, he told himself. If Jim Gage can find the right combination and zap this monster without killing me ...

"Hang in there, Mike," the doctor begged him when it got very bad. "Don't give up on me."

"I won't." Mike tried to smile. August, September, October. He made lists in his head and ticked off the items. He thought about his whitetail until he could almost see the thickness of its neck and shoulders, the royal sweep of its antlers out and forward, the tines clean and long, springing upward from the main branch. September, October. Could he make it in time? Doug visited every day and so did Mother and Dad, but it was alone that he pushed back the dark.

Then like a miracle the nightmare was over and he was back in the real world, almost as if it had never happened. Except it seemed that food tasted better and the sun was warmer and the sky bluer.

A secondary miracle, Mike passed grade eleven in spite of all the time he'd missed. In October he and Doug bought the last necessary supplies and crossed off the last items on the list. "The weekend of the teachers' conference?" Doug suggested, but Mike shook his head.

"Your dad will be planning to go with you then, and he'd never let me come along without checking with the parents first."

"You're really sure they won't let you go?"

"Surer than ever. It's early movies for me and in bed by ten."

"Jeez, it's a bummer."

Mike shrugged. "It's just the way they are. They mean well."

"I could get away the third weekend in November. I'm working every weekend until then."

Mike looked at the calendar and sucked his lower lip. The third weekend ... "I don't think so, Doug. Friday's the first of November. I could drive up early on the Saturday...."

"Alone?"

"You said you had to work."

"Yeah, but ..."

"I'll have the weekend, maybe stay a couple more days. It'll mean a big scene when I get back, but it'll be worth it."

"I wish you wouldn't go alone. You're only a beginner, and it's risky enough for anyone."

"I have to, Doug." Mike hesitated, feeling for the right words. "Three weeks to go. If I'm still okay by the 2nd, I think I should go then."

"I don't like it."

"Don't fuss. You sound like Mother and Dad."

It worked out like a dream. The parents went out to some party on Friday night. He didn't hear them come in, but he'd bet it was late. With luck they'd sleep till noon. Mike went to bed very early and set the alarm for five. It was one of the silent kind with a light that flashed off and on.

The first flash wakened him and he sat up at once, his mind clear and alert. He dressed quickly and quietly in the thermal undershirt and long johns that he'd bought secretly weeks before and hidden in the locked drawer of his desk. Jeans. A lightweight wool shirt with a mackinaw over that, a garish checked thing with four big useful pockets including one especially for cartridges. His downfill was in the hall closet, likewise his boots. He took time to roll a blanket lengthways and arrange it under the bedclothes in a realistic curve, punching up one of the pillows and then drawing up the covers. Most artistic. You'd swear he was asleep under that. He left a note, just a short one, so they wouldn't think he'd been kidnapped or anything.

He was itching to be gone, but he made himself take a minute to check his pockets. Driver's licence. Wildlife certificate.... He'd picked up the booklet at the shopping centre two weeks before, and already it was worn with being looked at so often. The accompanying tag he had buttoned carefully into the right breast pocket of his mackinaw. Even handling it made his heart thump. It was all beginning to become real at last....

The tag was just a simple metal strip with the same number stamped on it that was on his authorization certificate. Once he had killed a deer, *his* deer, he would have to wrap the metal tag around one of its antlers and fasten it shut. The clip fastening was irreversible. It could not be removed except by being cut off. Only one tag accompanied each authorization, and woe betide the hunter who was caught with untagged, unauthorized game. It reminded him of something quite different, Mike thought, and frowned, fishing for the memory. The hospital tag, that was it, that was wrapped around your wrist when you were admitted and only cut off when you left.

Time was going by. He unlocked the gun cabinet that

Dad had bought for him, carefully removed his rifle, and got a box of cartridges from the desk drawer. The rifle must go in a travelling case, he remembered. It was illegal to travel with a naked firearm. He slipped it into its case, took a last look around. That was it then.

He picked up his backpack and, with the gun case in the other hand, he opened the door of his room, sidled out and shut it carefully behind him. On socked feet he went past his parents' room and across the living room to the front door. He backtracked to the freezer in the kitchen and took out a package of T-bone steaks and pushed them into the pocket of his pack. Then he laced up his boots and pushed his arms into his downfill. At 5:30 in the morning, the second day of November, there'd be a real bite in the air.

He eased open the front door, holding his breath. It had a tendency to squeak. Then he closed it softly behind him and checked to see that the latch had caught. There. He was off!

He walked down the block rather quickly, with a distinct sense of relief when the curve of the crescent hid him from the windows of the house. He kept wanting to look back over his shoulder, even to start running. Then he imagined what sort of reaction he'd get from a passing police patrol, galloping along the street in the pre-dawn with a rifle tucked under one arm. He forced himself to walk at a deliberate pace, like a person who knew exactly what he was doing and where he was going and had nothing nefarious on his mind.

In a few minutes he'd be at the pick-up. The spade work

had all been done the night before. Doug had borrowed the pickup from his Dad with a story of camping out with a couple of guys from the Gun Club after work. Mike had dropped by to "help" him, and together they had loaded the truck with the new tent, Mike's sleeping bag – both of them smuggled out of Mike's house earlier in the week – an air mattress and an axe belonging to Doug's dad.

Doug's dad had come along just as they were loading up. He was on his way to work, on the night shift at one of the oil refineries east of the city. "Hope you'll be able to go along soon, Mike," he had said cheerily. "How's it going?"

"Pretty good, Mr. O'Reilly. Yeah, I'll be out in the bush in no time, I'm sure."

"Good for you. Goodnight, boys." He had waved and backed his battered old Chevy wagon out onto the street.

There was an awkward silence after he'd gone. In the end Mike broke it. "It's even worse telling lies to him, he's such a decent guy."

"It's all in a good cause," Doug said cheerfully enough, but Mike noticed that his ears had gone red.

"Will he give you heck when he finds out?"

"Probably. I mean, I wouldn't expect him not to. But don't worry about it. I can handle it, and he's not one to bear a grudge. Come on. I think we've got everything. Let's just check over the list one more time. Tent, bag, mattress, axe, rope …"

Doug had driven the pickup over to the shopping centre close to Mike's house and left it in the parking lot. It was quite dark and there were a few wispy clouds. The lot was empty and the two boys climbed out and stood looking at each other for a minute.

"Well, you'd better take the keys." Doug handed them over.

"Thanks. For everything. You know." Mike put them in his pocket.

"Looks like good weather." Doug glanced up at the sky.

"Yeah. Nice and clear. Good hunting weather, I guess."

"Yeah." Doug shuffled his feet against the pavement, kicked away a loose stone. "It could change fast though. Look, Mike, take care. Remember all the stuff we learned."

"I will. It'll be okay."

"It better be. If you kill yourself up there ..."

"Don't worry, I'll be careful. And look, it's not your fault anyway. I mean, I had to do this, one way or another. You just helped make it possible."

"Good luck then." Doug suddenly stuck out his hand. Mike shook it self-consciously. They'd never shaken hands before, in eleven years of being friends. It made everything suddenly official and solemn, like going off to war. "You'll get that trophy, Mike. I've got a good feeling about it."

"Me too. Thanks, Doug."

It was difficult to leave. He rattled the keys in his pocket and then turned away across the parking lot. Doug left in the opposite direction. They both turned when they came to the Street. Waved.

Good old Doug, Mike thought again at 5:35 in the morning of the first Saturday in November, walking down blue-lit streets towards the shopping centre. The pickup was there, just where Doug had parked it. Mike had had an irrational twinge of fear that somehow it might have vanished overnight. But there it was, tan-coloured, square and businesslike, sparkling with frost under the blue lights.

Mike unlocked the back and stowed away the rifle and the backpack. He climbed in front and started the engine, letting it idle to give it a chance to warm up while he scraped the frost off the windows. Then he climbed in again, shucked off his downfill and left it on the passenger seat. He fastened his seat belt and drove across the parking lot to the street. Then he turned left towards the Yellowhead Highway, for Barrhead, Fort Assiniboine and the Swan Hills.

NINE

Mike stared down at the hoofprints of the big whitetail cleanly stamped in the fresh snow. Nearly ten ... he'd been following it for hours. It should be off in the brush somewhere by now, chewing its cud. The sun slanted between the closely growing trees, providing a meagre amount of warmth. The deer would seek out a warm patch, he thought.

The air was still. It was the fourth day of the hunting season and he hadn't heard a single human sound since he'd made his camp two days ago, unless you counted the sound of the occasional plane arcing high across the wide cold emptiness of the sky. There was nothing for the deer to get edgy about. Nothing at all, except his presence.

He wished Doug were here. With two of them working together they could have planned a neat encircling movement, one of them going around and down into the next valley, so that his scent would drift up to the deer and send it back towards the other one, who'd be ready for it.

But he was on his own. Up to now he'd wanted it that

way. He chewed his lip and thought out alternatives. He could find a good "hide" and sit it out patiently until the deer came uptrail towards the cut for the evening browse. Probably that's what your topnotch woodsman would do....

Or he could go on down the trail and hope to surprise the buck at rest and get a good shot in time. There'd be the real risk that the whitetail – it was no fool, that big one – would become aware of what he was doing, and would drift on ahead of him, always just out of range, until Mike was either lost or exhausted or both. But in spite of all these obvious disadvantages this was what he wanted to do. There'd been altogether too much waiting around in his life recently, Mike decided. It was time for him to make a move.

He drifted down the trail, five or six steps at a time, pausing to scan as far ahead and to the left and right as he could through the densely packed trees, then raking the middle ground with his eyes, looking low for the partial glimpse of a great antler among dead tree branches which spiked up antler-like everywhere, and for the curve of a grey shoulder in a world of grey shadows.

Just how well could a deer as big as this one hide in this kind of brush? There was little dense growth between the trees, as little light came in. But there was plenty of deadfall. Whenever a storm knocked down an old tree others would fall in a domino effect. It was in these tangled areas of trunks and dry branches that he must look for the daytime resting place of his whitetail.

He moved carefully on. A squirrel chittered restlessly

not far away. He wasn't angry yet, just a bit bothered. Mike froze and held his breath. There was a scuttering in the branches high above his head and to the left. All right, all right, I'm going, he muttered to himself, and moved on out of the squirrel's territory.

The deer run looped from left to right around natural obstacles, but in general Mike found that he was moving downhill and at the same time westward, deeper into the hills. There were many other trails here. They crisscrossed, ran parallel for a while, and crisscrossed again; but in spite of their wanderings it seemed that all of them were leading westwards and downwards. His buck's hoofprints were still distinguishable among the others, deeper and larger, clearly imprinted in the snow. Slowly, painstakingly, Mike worked his way deeper into the forest.

It must have been almost noon – the sun was about twenty-five degrees above the horizon, and due south – when it seemed to him that the trees were beginning to thin out. He had glimpses of large patches of sky, clear blue and cloudless. It was getting warmer too, now that the sun's rays could penetrate between the spruce and pine and heat up the ground a little. Was he coming to another cut? Funny place to find it, though, near the bottom of a valley....

He moved forward with even greater caution. There was less cover now. Six steps. Pause. Scan left to right far ground. Then middle. Finally close. Before long he came to a place where there seemed to *be* no middle ground. It didn't make sense; then he saw that he was looking across a narrow defile towards a northfacing flank of hill, a carbon copy of the slope he was on.

For a moment he had that strange feeling that he had followed this trail before, that he was going round and round in circles. He had an instant's dry-mouthed panic as he realized just how fatally easy it would be to get completely lost among these gentle tree-choked slopes, each one exactly like the one on cither side of it....

He licked his dry lips and reminded himself firmly that he had taken a compass-bearing of the direction back to the Freeman River and his camp. There was no way he could get lost, except by losing his head. Don't panic, he told himself. You're in control. He was all right. He knew where he was, and what he was doing. He knew how he'd got there, and how to get out again. He told himself this until his heart stopped pounding. Then he moved forward again until there was only a single file of trees separating him from the open ground beyond.

He could see the dazzle of sunlight, lying golden across a tangle of small sapling growth, wispy aspens and conifers like miniature Christmas trees, knee-high, decorated with scallops of snow. Somewhere in the midst of the tangle was the very faint sound of running water. A week ago Mike would not have been able to hear that tiny sound, but for two days now his ears had become more finely tuned, with nothing louder than the song of a chickadee, the scolding of squirrel and Canada jay, and the noise of his own breath and blood.

He stood very still and tried to quieten his breathing now. He was looking into the bottom of a tiny valley, with no river like the Freeman, but some unmapped stream, unimportant to anyone but the animals who came down here to drink.

Very slowly, with the minimum of movement, he raised his rifle and used the scope to survey the area below and to his right. He very nearly skimmed right past the small patch of grey. It was so very small, so insignificant. He had passed it by when some unanswered question in the back of his mind made him hesitate and move back again.

He was just in time to see the great head come up and gaze around. He was able to count the tines, to calculate the width between the two great curves of the main branches. His heart was pounding so loudly that he could hear it, and his ears felt woolly, the way they feel when you're taking off in a jet. Mike swallowed, got his hearing back, and tried to force himself to breathe slowly, calmly.

Oh, you beauty! He stared at it through the scope. The head remained up, alert. Could it see him? Scent him? The ears twitched once, forward and back. Then the head moved down again towards the water, out of his line of sight.

Very, very gently, Mike moved the bolt handle forward and down. The bolt was now locked against the chamber, sealing in the cartridge. The sear above the trigger automatically engaged the notch on the head of the firing pin. The rifle was now cocked, ready to fire. The whole series of actions made one small, faintly audible click.

Mike was sighting down the scope when the whitetail's head came up again. He froze.... There was a light breeze coming up out of the valley. He could feel it cold against his forehead. He hadn't realized that he was sweating. His eyes swam and clouded his view. He squeezed them shut, stared again. That was better.

His buck was alert, but not yet anxious. Mike felt as if there were a fine thread, as thin and tenuous as a flying spider's filament, joining him to the deer. He knew with certainty that it wasn't going to drink again. It was going to move away. But not in a hurry. It was not spooked, only uneasy.

He moved the rifle slowly downwards to the left, until he was looking through the scope at the mass of shoulder muscle. Now at last he had arrived at his moment of glory. The forefinger of his right hand delicately felt the trigger. Just one squeeze – how many grams of pressure? Very little and the whole mechanism of destruction would be set in motion. The sear would disengage from the notch on the firing pin and the spring of the bolt would force the firing pin against the exact centre of the base of the cartridge, thus detonating the primer and, almost instantly, the powder. The ignited powder would then expand to fill the sealed chamber with hot gases, forcing the bullet from the end of the cartridge down the rifle barrel.

At a distance of a hundred metres the bullet would have travelled to that spot on the shoulder of the buck marked by the cross-hairs of his scope before his brain was even aware of the noise of the exploding cartridge. A cartridge loaded with a hundred grains of powder would send his bullet speeding at 770 metres per second to smack into the deer, tearing through the shoulder muscle, penetrating lung tissue, perhaps even the heart, its soft tip spreading, mushrooming, to cause massive internal bleeding.

The whitetail had no chance at all against his steady hand and eye. He couldn't possibly miss. It was the trophy of his dreams. No, it was better than his dreams. It was bigger, it was three-dimensional. It was real.

His finger felt the trigger. In five minutes it would all be over and he would be down at the bottom of that sunny little valley. He would be taking the tag from his pocket and wrapping it around one of the main branches of those mighty antlers. Then, at last, it would be *his*.

Imagining the soft metal band, hearing in his mind's ear the faint click as the tag end was pushed through the fastening, he had an instant of total recall. He was back in Admitting. It was his third visit, and the odds against him were climbing steadily. The nurse clipped around his wrist the plastic tag with his name embossed on it. MICHAEL RANKIN. He had looked down at it, that badge of slavery, and he had wondered with despair when it would be cut off. If ... did they bury you with your tag still attached? Oh, God, God, it isn't fair! Why me? ...

Very gently Mike's forefinger disengaged from the trigger. He moved the rifle up and to the right again, until the whitetail's head was again centred in the scope. You're mine, he told his trophy deer, you're all mine. And for today

I'm God. Quickly, violently, before he could change his mind, he slammed the bolt handle up.

As the bolt head disengaged from the barrel chamber, a notch at the bottom of the bolt handle caught the protruding finger of the firing-pin head, pushing the firing pin back from the centre base of the cartridge. There was a loud click. It seemed to Mike that that click echoed round the world, that the whole universe had stilled, waiting for his decision.

Then time began to run smoothly forward again, like the stream Mike could hear whispering between its ice-encrusted banks. He could hear the shiver of dead aspen leaves that still clung to the saplings clustered along the banks of the stream. A long way off there was a chitter of squirrels.

The whitetail snorted. Mike could see the little puff of vapour from its nostrils. Its white tail flickered up, exposing its white rump. The ears twitched and were laid back. Then, in one glorious effortless leap, the buck cleared the stream and five metres of brush. There was a noise of breaking and bending saplings. Then the whitetail was gone, vanishing like smoke into the shadow of the trees on the south side of the valley.

Mike lowered his gun and walked slowly down through the low brush until he found the stream, ice-encrusted. He squatted down to drink. It was cold and very sweet, as new as Paradise. It took only a little to quench his thirst. Then he moved away until he found a small sandy patch, blown nearly clear of snow, warm in the sun. Here he sat to eat a cheese sandwich and a granola bar.

When he had eaten he went back for another drink, more to taste the cleanness of the water than because he was thirsty. He stretched up with his arms above his head and breathed in the clear cold air. It was wonderful to be alive.

He took a careful compass bearing, due east, and then he headed off uphill again. It had taken him from six in the morning until early afternoon to find his buck and stalk it up the flank of one hill and down into the next valley. It took no more than two hours to get back to his camp, walking at a comfortable pace along the deer runs, stopping only when he felt like it, to smell the spicy smell of spruce gum warmed by the sun, to admire a cluster of bright bunchberries blown clear of snow.

He lit his fire one last time and set his coffee pan to boil, and put the frying pan with a big steak in it sizzling in the hottest part of the fire. While it was cooking he struck his tent and folded it and packed it up, and piled his other belongings ready to carry to the pickup.

Would he be out this way again? If not, well, he'd got *this* time to remember. He stretched out his hands to the fire and the cuffs of his mackinaw fell back, exposing his wrists, still rather pale and skinny. He warmed his hands at the blaze. Against the light you could almost see the outline of the bones, the pinkiness of blood coursing through his body.

The road he was on wasn't an either-or road, he had discovered. He wasn't going towards either life or death. That wasn't what it was all about, he'd got it wrong all this time. It was on *through* life towards death, which had to be there at the end, or else life itself would become as flat as bread without yeast, as tasteless as a wiener without mustard.

When his steak was finished and the scraps thrown into the fire, and he had had his last lingering cup of coffee, hot, sweet and faintly smoky – if they could only bottle that true bush flavour they'd make a fortune, he thought – Mike began to haul his belongings along the trail to the pickup.

On the last trip he stopped to put out the fire, scattering it well, scraping the frozen dirt over it, and some snow for good measure. Now it was as if he had never been there, except for the square, snowless patch where his tent had stood. The sun had set just before five and it was now seven. He'd be home by ten-thirty.

Overhead the sky was dark and the stars were strengthening one by one, filling the sky with their comfortingly familiar patterns. He picked up the backpack and the rifle and took a last look round.

Now that the fire was out the dark crept forward from its hiding places among the trees and filled the clearing. It pressed closely against him as he trudged along the familiar trail that skirted the river. The dark didn't bother him any more. In fact it was comforting. He and the dark had met in that long instant when he had looked through the 4X Bushnell scope at his trophy whitetail buck. Face to face he had recognized it, and known that the enemy from whom he had been running for so long was in fact his friend.

ABOUT THE AUTHOR

Monica Hughes, a writer of international acclaim, was born in Liverpool, England in 1925. She immigrated to Canada in 1952, eventually settling in Edmonton, Alberta. She had always wanted to write but did not publish her first book, *Gold-Fever Trail* until 1974. In a prolific career that spanned twenty-nine years, she went on to write over thirty five books, and many short stories and articles. She was often honored for her work; *Hunter in the Dark* and *Keeper of the Isis Light* both won the Canada Council Children's Literature Award. She was the recipient of the Vicky Metcalfe Award for a body of work, the Queen's Jubilee Medal, and the Order of Canada. Published in over ten languages, she also received international honors, including the Silver Feather Award and the Phoenix Award.

Monica once said she had so many plots buzzing around in her head that sometimes she felt her mind was an airport with ideas instead of planes stacked up and waiting to land. Best known for her science fiction titles, she also wrote award-winning picture books, beginner readers, and historical and modern fiction. She died in March 2003.